OPPOSING
VIEWPOINTS®
SERIES

WITHDRAWN

| Mass Shootings

Other Books of Related Interest

Opposing Viewpoints Series

Gun Violence
Mass Incarceration
Violent Video Games and Society

At Issue Series

Are Graphic Music Lyrics Harmful?
Domestic Terrorism
Guns: Conceal and Carry

Current Controversies Series

America's Mental Health Crisis
Homelessness and Street Crime
School Violence

> "Congress shall make no law ... abridging the freedom of speech, or of the press."

First Amendment to the US Constitution

The basic foundation of our democracy is the First Amendment guarantee of freedom of expression. The Opposing Viewpoints series is dedicated to the concept of this basic freedom and the idea that it is more important to practice it than to enshrine it.

OPPOSING
VIEWPOINTS®
SERIES

| Mass Shootings

Martin Gitlin, Book Editor

GREENHAVEN
PUBLISHING

Published in 2021 by Greenhaven Publishing, LLC
353 3rd Avenue, Suite 255, New York, NY 10010

Articles in Greenhaven Publishing anthologies are often edited for length to meet page
requirements. In addition, original titles of these works are changed to clearly present
the main thesis and to explicitly indicate the author's opinion. Every effort is made to
ensure that Greenhaven Publishing accurately reflects the original intent of the authors.
Every effort has been made to trace the owners of the copyrighted material.

Cover image: David Becker/Getty Images

Library of Congress Cataloging-in-Publication Data
Names: Gitlin, Marty, editor.
Title: Mass shootings / Martin Gitlin, editor.
Description: New York : Greenhaven Publishing, 2021. | Series: Opposing
    viewpoints | Includes bibliographical references and index. | Audience: Grades 9–12.
Identifiers: LCCN 2020000073 | ISBN 9781534506893 (library binding) | ISBN
    9781534506886 (paperback)
Subjects: LCSH: Mass shootings—United States. | Mass shootings—United
    States—Prevention. | Firearms and crime—United States. | Gun
    control—United States. | Violence in mass media—United States.
Classification: LCC HM866 .M197 2020 | DDC 363.330973—dc23
LC record available at https://lccn.loc.gov/2020000073

Manufactured in the United States of America

Website: http://greenhavenpublishing.com

Contents

Chapter 3: How Important Is the Second Amendment?

Chapter 4: How Should the Problem of Mass Shootings Be Addressed?

The Importance of Opposing Viewpoints

Perhaps every generation experiences a period in time in which the populace seems especially polarized, starkly divided on the important issues of the day and gravitating toward the far ends of the political spectrum and away from a consensus-facilitating middle ground. The world that today's students are growing up in and that they will soon enter into as active and engaged citizens is deeply fragmented in just this way. Issues relating to terrorism, immigration, women's rights, minority rights, race relations, health care, taxation, wealth and poverty, the environment, policing, military intervention, the proper role of government—in some ways, perennial issues that are freshly and uniquely urgent and vital with each new generation—are currently roiling the world.

If we are to foster a knowledgeable, responsible, active, and engaged citizenry among today's youth, we must provide them with the intellectual, interpretive, and critical-thinking tools and experience necessary to make sense of the world around them and of the all-important debates and arguments that inform it. After all, the outcome of these debates will in large measure determine the future course, prospects, and outcomes of the world and its peoples, particularly its youth. If they are to become successful members of society and productive and informed citizens, students need to learn how to evaluate the strengths and weaknesses of someone else's arguments, how to sift fact from opinion and fallacy, and how to test the relative merits and validity of their own opinions against the known facts and the best possible available information. The landmark series Opposing Viewpoints has been providing students with just such critical-thinking skills and exposure to the debates surrounding society's most urgent contemporary issues for many years, and it continues to serve this essential role with undiminished commitment, care, and rigor.

The key to the series's success in achieving its goal of sharpening students' critical-thinking and analytic skills resides in its title—

Opposing Viewpoints. In every intriguing, compelling, and engaging volume of this series, readers are presented with the widest possible spectrum of distinct viewpoints, expert opinions, and informed argumentation and commentary, supplied by some of today's leading academics, thinkers, analysts, politicians, policy makers, economists, activists, change agents, and advocates. Every opinion and argument anthologized here is presented objectively and accorded respect. There is no editorializing in any introductory text or in the arrangement and order of the pieces. No piece is included as a "straw man," an easy ideological target for cheap point-scoring. As wide and inclusive a range of viewpoints as possible is offered, with no privileging of one particular political ideology or cultural perspective over another. It is left to each individual reader to evaluate the relative merits of each argument—as he or she sees it, and with the use of ever-growing critical-thinking skills—and grapple with his or her own assumptions, beliefs, and perspectives to determine how convincing or successful any given argument is and how the reader's own stance on the issue may be modified or altered in response to it.

This process is facilitated and supported by volume, chapter, and selection introductions that provide readers with the essential context they need to begin engaging with the spotlighted issues, with the debates surrounding them, and with their own perhaps shifting or nascent opinions on them. In addition, guided reading and discussion questions encourage readers to determine the authors' point of view and purpose, interrogate and analyze the various arguments and their rhetoric and structure, evaluate the arguments' strengths and weaknesses, test their claims against available facts and evidence, judge the validity of the reasoning, and bring into clearer, sharper focus the reader's own beliefs and conclusions and how they may differ from or align with those in the collection or those of their classmates.

Research has shown that reading comprehension skills improve dramatically when students are provided with compelling, intriguing, and relevant "discussable" texts. The subject matter of these collections could not be more compelling, intriguing, or urgently relevant to today's students and the world they are poised to inherit. The anthologized articles and the reading and discussion questions that are included with them also provide the basis for stimulating, lively, and passionate classroom debates. Students who are compelled to anticipate objections to their own argument and identify the flaws in those of an opponent read more carefully, think more critically, and steep themselves in relevant context, facts, and information more thoroughly. In short, using discussable text of the kind provided by every single volume in the Opposing Viewpoints series encourages close reading, facilitates reading comprehension, fosters research, strengthens critical thinking, and greatly enlivens and energizes classroom discussion and participation. The entire learning process is deepened, extended, and strengthened.

For all of these reasons, Opposing Viewpoints continues to be exactly the right resource at exactly the right time—when we most need to provide readers with the critical-thinking tools and skills that will not only serve them well in school but also in their careers and their daily lives as decision-making family members, community members, and citizens. This series encourages respectful engagement with and analysis of opposing viewpoints and fosters a resulting increase in the strength and rigor of one's own opinions and stances. As such, it helps make readers "future ready," and that readiness will pay rich dividends for the readers themselves, for the citizenry, for our society, and for the world at large.

Introduction

"In the decade between 2009 and 2018, the horrific scenes of mass shootings have haunted the nation's collective conscience. Each breaking news alert floods the nation with grief and anger at this senseless, preventable violence. The United States is not the only country with mental illness, domestic violence, or hate-fueled ideologies, but our gun homicide rate is 25 times higher than other high-income countries."

—Everytown for Gun Safety, November 21, 2019

A healthy perspective is required before one debates the wide range of concerns and possible solutions to the horrific mass shootings that have plagued the United States for a generation. That outlook must be for everyone to acknowledge that all Americans seek the same goal, ultimately. And that is for the violence to stop.

How can it be made to stop, or at least slowed to a far less alarming rate? Therein lies the rub. The answers cannot be found only in arguments and discussions. Most people, regardless of their political persuasion, understand that both the government at all levels and the people it serves must take concrete steps to curb or ideally end the spate of tragedies.

And that means making decisions. The problem is that there is little agreement on many issues. There is too much gray area on too many questions. Why are so many people prone to mass murder in modern American society? Is it strictly a mental health issue? Would stronger gun control laws solve the problem, or are some people determined to kill by hook or by crook? Is there a happy medium with an assault weapons ban? Can bad guys with guns only be stopped by good guys with guns? Why are nearly all mass shootings perpetrated by men? And why are so many done by young men in schools?

There are no clear answers to any of those questions. But something must be done. And one thing most Americans agree upon is that their leaders are not doing enough. They have not even achieved what a huge majority of the country believe is necessary. That is passing laws that mandate far stronger background checks for gun purchases. Millions of people frustrated with the government cite that failure as evidence of its inaction.

There is indeed gray area in every debate.

One can assume that a huge majority of mass shooters are plagued with mental issues. But evidence varies. Can society be assured that such problems and the evil motives of potentially dangerous people be consistently identified in time for tragedies to be avoided? Friends and relatives of mass murderers have often stated their wonderment that people they knew could have committed such heinous acts.

That leads to spirited discussions over gun control. It is the vaguest aspect of the debate. What would the most effective means of gun control entail? Some believe universal background checks would be sufficient. Others feel assault weapons, which have been used often in mass shootings, must be banned. The most vigilant among gun control advocates insist on buybacks and a plan that would remove all guns from private hands.

Those that consider themselves realists and pragmatists argue the opposite. They claim that criminal activity cannot be halted by law. They state that those seeking to kill will find a way. They will go underground to purchase weapons. Those against gun control measures also cite the millions of guns already in the streets as proof that they are readily available. Why, they ask, would anyone with intent to kill—the most heinous of all crimes—consider the law when planning such sinister deeds?

Gun control supporters point an accusing finger at those holding such opinions. They offer that people who back gun rights have no solutions beyond providing more guns for "good people" and the blurry notion of stopping those deemed dangerous from procuring a weapon. And though more Americans have strengthened the radar that identifies potential mass shooters, thereby preventing tragedy, depending solely on the vigilance of others is far from a foolproof plan.

And what about the Second Amendment? How should that be interpreted? Must a document written more than two centuries ago, when people carried around muskets, be considered unbreakable? Should the amendment be altered or scrapped? Or must Americans and their leaders continue to debate how it should be interpreted in the modern world? Does the Second Amendment not identify the need for a well-regulated militia as the motivation for gun rights? And how does that relate to a twenty-first century in which people can kill hundreds in seconds with assault weapons?

The "good guy with guns" debate also grows more heated. President Donald Trump went so far as to suggest that teachers should be armed and trained to shoot in classrooms. Backers of such a plan believe that the only way to stop mass shootings is to arm as many "good" people as possible. Those that argue against that notion cite that people will die before the good shooter eliminates the bad shooter. Assault weapons can kill dozens before the perpetrator can be identified and gunned down. Good guys with guns, therefore, is only a partial solution that will still leave many dead. And one can claim that it is unfair to depend on anyone but trained police officers to defend the public with guns.

The arguments grow more heated with every tragedy in schools or churches or malls. But then they fade. Government officials and other Americans offer thoughts and prayers to the victims and their families. And soon they all go on with their lives. Nothing gets done. The voices of those that continue to fight for a solution are lost in the wilderness.

When will strong and lasting steps be taken to stem the tide of mass shootings? And what will that action entail? Only time will tell. And most people believe that time is of the essence, especially for the still unknown victims who will lose their lives suddenly and tragically when the next mass shooting occurs.

The complicated and often emotional arguments surrounding this topic are represented in *Opposing Viewpoints: Mass Shootings*. In chapters titled "Why Are There So Many Mass Shootings?"; "Are Guns the Root of the Problem?"; How Important Is the Second Amendment?"; and "How Should the Problem of Mass Shootings Be Addresssed?", viewpoint authors explore different facets of this phenomenon and offer solutions to decreasing the number of incidents in the future.

CHAPTER 1

Why Are There So Many Mass Shootings?

Chapter Preface

A one-word question has been asked repeatedly since two disturbed young men murdered thirteen classmates in Columbine High School in 1999, setting off a spate of mass killings that has spanned an entire generation. That question: Why?

Why has America been shaken by so many of these tragedies? What has motivated people—many of them mere children—to procure weapons and take innocent lives? In many cases, after all, the victims were unknown to the perpetrators.

The following chapter examines that vexing issue. But the reality is there is not one answer. Shooters have been driven by a wide range of motives and influences. The problem with this fact is that it makes it harder to emerge with a solution to mass shootings. And it results in debates with no clear answer.

Perhaps violent video games have caused some to embark on shooting rampages. Bullying, both in person and online, certainly seems to have triggered young people to pull triggers. Other violent acts have been followed with shoulder shrugs. Nobody figured out why a wealthy man murdered 59 and injured more than 500 from a hotel window in Las Vegas in 2017. There were simply no explanations.

Motivations are individual. No two cases are exactly alike. One can argue that common factors in mass shootings, such as bullying or violence in the media, provide a basis for emerging with more concrete steps to prevent such tragedies. Campaigns against bullying, for instance, have been strengthened in recent years. But the very personal reasons for committing mass murder, such as simple revenge for perceived mistreatment, means there is no one solution.

The result is a wide-ranging debate. Some believe it is best to accept that angry or disturbed people might go off and that focus should be put on keeping weapons of mass destruction out of their hands. Others feel it is essential to prevent the causes of evil intent. The perspectives in this chapter explore both angles.

> *"Although the issue is often presented as controversial in the media, we have pretty good evidence that exposure to violent media does make children more aggressive. And we've known it for decades."*

Violence in Media Creates Violence in Children

Vanessa LoBue

In the following viewpoint, Vanessa LoBue cites studies that prove a link between violence in the media and violent action taken by kids. Her argument is that such violent tendencies perpetrated by the media can be especially problematic when combined with the availability of guns. The author suggests that children should be shielded from violence in the media if parents hope to ensure they will grow up with a healthy respect for the safety of others. Vanessa LoBue is an associate professor of psychology at Rutgers University-Newark who specializes in infant and child psychology.

"Violent Media and Aggressive Behavior in Children," by Vanessa LoBue Ph.D, Sussex Publishers, LLC, January 8, 2018. Reprinted by permission.

As you read, consider the following questions:

1. Why do some experts reject links between violence in the media and violent behavior among kids, and others do not?
2. Does the author's use of studies involving kids make her argument successful?
3. Children have been exposed to media violence for decades. Why do you believe it has resulted in disturbingly violent behavior only recently?

With recent worry about mass shootings and gun violence in the US, one of the questions that always comes up is whether violent media promotes violent or aggressive behavior. This is something that is especially important to think about for parents, as violent content is common on television and in movies, on the Internet, and in some of the most popular children's video games.

Although the issue is often presented as controversial in the media, we have pretty good evidence that exposure to violent media does make children more aggressive. And we've known it for decades. In one of the most well-known studies on this topic (published back in the 1960s), researchers showed preschoolers a video of an adult playing with an inflatable doll. In the video, the children watched as the adult sat on the doll, punched it in the nose, hit the doll on the head with a mallet, and kicked it repeatedly. After watching the video, the children were brought into a playroom with the same doll and lots of other toys.

As predicted, the kids who watched the aggressive video imitated what they saw—they beat the doll with a mallet, and they punched and kicked it. What was most surprising was that the children found new and creative ways to beat up the doll, and they played more aggressively with the other toys in the room as well. Children didn't just imitate the aggressive behaviors they

WHAT ARE THE CONNECTIONS BETWEEN BULLYING AND SCHOOL SHOOTINGS?

Almost every individual thinks that every school shooter is that weird kid that got bullied on a daily basis. The reason behind this perspective is the sheer number of articles that make this connection without any relevant data that can back-up those claims.

Same goes with mental problems in shooters, and according to many "so-called" news sites, every other school shooter had a mental illness no one paid attention to. This type of info is hugely misleading. However, there are connections between bullying and mental illnesses with a school shooting, even though they aren't as common as people think.

There is no shame in admitting that we live in a society that frowns upon those that are different. Every class has a weird kid or two that don't fit into groups other students create. People don't realize that being different isn't bad and that every individual should be able to live as they want. Being quiet and not interested in things other people find fascinating is perfectly fine.

Now, bullying usually happens to quiet kids that don't fit into other groups in their classes. But that doesn't mean that every kid

saw; seeing aggressive behaviors caused these kids to play more aggressively in general (Bandura, Ross, & Ross, 1963).

Very recent research suggests that these effects can become particularly problematic when guns are involved. Researchers from Ohio State University brought pairs of 8- to 12-year-old children into a lab and showed them a 20-minute version of a popular PG-rated movie—either the *Rocketeer* (1991) or *National Treasure* (2004). In the edited movie, the children either saw that actual movie footage, which contained characters using guns, or they watched a version where the guns were edited out. They were then presented with a large room that contained various toys including Legos, Nerf guns, and games.

that gets bullied will choose to take a firearm and shoot others. This also doesn't mean that bullying is OK. Schools and parents should take steps to prevent this kind of activity from happening as it may lead to unfortunate events. A kid that is bullied might have a rough life outside of the school, and that kind of activity may push them over the line.

Claims that school shootings happen because individuals with mental issues can get guns without any issues are partially correct. But the problem is that the number of shooters that had severe psychological problems is negligible. The biggest problem is the combination of bullying and mental illness.

Kids nowadays are allowed to do anything they want, and thus they will bully someone even though they know that the individual is having problems. They think that actions they take won't have any repercussions which result in kids pouring bleach in mentally challenged eyes and similar things.

Once in a while, a kid that is bullied will bring a gun to a school and kill someone because their pleas reach no one. Making sure that bullying doesn't happen is hard, but that is one of the ways that will reduce the number of these tragedies.

"Bullying and Mass Shooting—Is There a Connection?" by Louis Stroup, Louis Stroup, January 20, 2018.

Not surprisingly, the children who watched the movie with the guns played more aggressively than children who watched the movie with the guns edited out, consistent with previous research.

But that wasn't all; the study had a bit of a twist. The playroom also contained a closed cabinet, wherein one of the drawers was a real 0.38-caliber handgun. The gun was not loaded, and it was modified so that it couldn't fire bullets. It was also modified so that it kept track of the number of times the trigger was pulled hard enough that the gun would have gone off.

The children weren't told that there was a gun in the room, the researchers were simply interested in whether the children would find the gun on their own, and if they did, what they'd do with it.

About 83 percent of the kids in the study found the gun, and most of them played with it. Of the kids who found it, 27 percent immediately gave it to the experimenter and the experimenter took it out of the room. Of the remaining 58 percent of kids who found the gun, 42 percent played with it in various ways. Importantly, almost none of the kids who watched the movie clip without guns ever pulled the trigger.

The kids who watched the movie that contained gun footage were more likely to pull the trigger of the real gun; on average, they pulled it about two to three times and spent four to five times longer holding it when compared to kids who watched the movie with no gun footage. What's scarier is that some of these kids pulled the trigger more than a few times; in fact, they pulled it quite a lot. Some pulled the trigger over 20 times; one child pointed the gun out the window at people walking down the street; and another child pressed the gun to another child's temple and pulled the trigger (Dillon, & Bushman, 2017).

This research suggests that violent media can cause aggressive behavior in children and that this behavior can be incredibly problematic if violent media includes guns. Indeed, children are incredibly curious about guns, and they can have difficulty understanding the difference between real and toy guns (Benjamin, Kepes, & Bushman, 2017).

In fact, there is research suggesting that guns don't need to be featured in the media to cause aggression; the mere presence of a gun is enough to elicit aggressive behavior. For example, having a gun sitting on a table makes people behave more aggressively (Berkowitz & LePage, 1967), and recent work shows that having a gun in the car makes people (even non-gun owners) more aggressive drivers (Bushman, Kerwin, Whitlock, & Weisenberger, 2017). These effects even exist in children, whether or not the gun is real or is just a toy (Benjamin Kepes, & Bushman, 2017).

So can viewing violent media cause more aggression in children? The answer based on this research is a very clear yes. And it's worth pointing out that the videos children saw in the studies I described were pretty mild; they either saw a homemade video of someone playing roughly with a doll, or 20-minute clips of movies that were rated PG. The violence in these videos pales in comparison to the violence in other full-length movies and in video games, which have also been linked to increases in aggressive behavior (Anderson & Bushman, 2001).

The clear implication from here is that if you don't want your children to be aggressive or violent, keep them away from violent media, and even away from toy weapons that might encourage aggressive behavior all on their own. That doesn't mean you won't end up with an aggressive child—some children are just naturally more aggressive than others—but it's certainly a start.

References

Anderson, C. A., & Bushman, B. J. (2001). Effects of violent video games on aggressive behavior, aggressive cognition, aggressive affect, physiological arousal, and prosocial behavior: A meta-analytic review of the scientific literature. *Psychological Science*, 12, 353-359.

Bandura, A., Ross, D., & Ross, S. A. (1963). Imitation of film-mediated aggressive models. *The Journal of Abnormal and Social Psychology*, 66, 3-11.

Berkowitz, L., & LePage, A. (1967). Weapons as aggression-eliciting stimuli. *Journal of Personality and Social Psychology*, 7(2p1), 202-207.

Dillon, K. P., & Bushman, B. J. (2017, in press). Effects of Exposure to Gun Violence in Movies on Children's Interest in Real Guns. *JAMA pediatrics*.

Bushman, B. J., Kerwin, T., Whitlock, T., & Weisenberger, J. M. (2017). The weapons effect on wheels: Motorists drive more aggressively when there is a gun in the vehicle. *Journal of Experimental Social Psychology*, 73, 82-85.

Benjamin Jr, A. J., Kepes, S., & Bushman, B. J. (2017, in press). Effects of weapons on aggressive thoughts, angry feelings, hostile appraisals, and aggressive behavior: a meta-analytic review of the weapons effect literature. *Personality and Social Psychology Review*.

> "*The reality is that we have not yet successfully defined violence and aggression, whether when analyzing the content we consume, or investigating the potentially resultant aggressive behaviour.*"

Violent Media Does Not Create Mass Killers

MediaSmarts

In the following viewpoint, MediaSmarts objectively explores many aspects of media impact on young people. The authors argue that violent video games have been acknowledged as having some negative influences, but not to the extent that they can be blamed for mass shootings. The authors also touch upon the effects of violence in movies and television on children. They conclude that while the media contributes to aggressive behavior, one should look elsewhere for specific causes of such tragedies. MediaSmarts is a Canadian-based not-for-profit charitable organization for digital and media literacy.

"What Do We Know About Media Violence?" MediaSmarts. Reprinted by permission.

As you read, consider the following questions:

1. Why does this viewpoint stop short of blaming video games for mass shootings?
2. What do the authors claim to be negative influences of violent video games?
3. What do the authors say about the effects of the Internet on children?

It is difficult to set down in a definitive way what effect media violence has on consumers and young people. There are a number of reasons for this, but the main issue is that terms like "violence" and "aggression" are not easily defined or categorized. To a child, almost any kind of conflict, such as the heated arguments of some talk-radio shows or primetime news pundits, can sound as aggressive as two cartoon characters dropping anvils on one another.

The reality is that we have not yet successfully defined violence and aggression, whether when analyzing the content we consume, or investigating the potentially resultant aggressive behaviour. Because individual studies define these notions differently, the goal posts are constantly moving for anyone who is trying to get a big picture look at the situation. The difficulty of quantifying aggression and violence in a strict way makes it nearly impossible to accurately answer the question "Does media violence cause people to commit violence?"

Many Studies, Many Conclusions

Back in 1994 Andrea Martinez at the University of Ottawa conducted a comprehensive review of the scientific literature on media violence for the Canadian Radio-television and Telecommunications Commission (CRTC). She concluded that the lack of consensus about media effects reflects three "grey areas" or constraints contained in the research itself. These grey areas still apply today.

First, media violence is notoriously hard to define and measure. Some experts who track violence in television programming, such as the late George Gerbner, defined violence as the act (or threat) of injuring or killing someone, independent of the method used or the surrounding context. As such, Gerber included cartoon violence in his data-set. But others, such as University of Laval professors Guy Paquette and Jacques de Guise, specifically excluded cartoon violence from their research because of its comical and unrealistic presentation. (How they would view some of the increasingly realistic violence in many of today's cartoons aimed at teens—such as the gruesome injuries suffered by many of the characters on South Park and Family Guy—is an open question.)

Second, researchers disagree over the type of relationship the data supports. Some argue that exposure to media violence causes aggression. Others say that the two are associated, but that there is no causal connection (that both, for instance, may be caused by some third factor) while others say the data supports the conclusion that there is no relationship between the two at all.

Third, even those who agree that there is a connection between media violence and aggression disagree about how the one affects the other. Some say that the mechanism is a psychological one, rooted in the ways we learn. For example, L. Rowell Huesmann argues that children develop "cognitive scripts" that guide their own behaviour by imitating the actions of media heroes. As they watch violent shows, children learn to internalize scripts that use violence as an appropriate method of problem-solving.

Other researchers argue that it is the physiological effects of media violence that cause aggressive behaviour. Exposure to violent imagery is linked to increased heart rate, faster respiration and higher blood pressure. Some think that this simulated "fight-or-flight" response predisposes people to act aggressively in the real world.

Still others focus on the ways in which media violence primes or cues pre-existing aggressive thoughts and feelings. They argue that an individual's desire to strike out is justified by media images in which both the hero and the villain use violence to seek revenge, often without consequences.

In her final report to the CRTC, Martinez concluded that most studies support "a positive, though weak, relation between exposure to television violence and aggressive behaviour." Although that relationship cannot be "confirmed systematically," she agrees with Dutch researcher Tom Van der Voot who argues that it would be illogical to conclude that "a phenomenon does not exist simply because it is found at times not to occur, or only to occur under certain circumstances."

With that in mind, based on a number of recent studies published in peer-reviewed academic journals, there are some things we *can* say:

What's the good news?

- Violent video games are not causally related to incidents like high school shootings.[1]
- Video games are not causally linked to youth crime, aggression, and dating violence.[2]
- Violent video games have not led to an increase in violent crime; in fact, violent crime has decreased in the years since game playing became a common activity for youth.[3]
- Even though consumers tend to gravitate towards violent media, we are generally more satisfied by and take more joy from non-violent media.[4]

What's the bad news?

- Violent video games may desensitize players to other violent images and emotional stimuli.[5]
- Violent media often portray violent acts and situations but rarely represent the consequences of violence.[6]
- Violent video games may lead to increased aggression in some young children and youth by making aggression seem like a reasonable response to everyday conflicts.[7]

What else needs to be considered?

- Despite the emphasis placed on the possibility of violent media as a risk factor for youth violence, there are a number of far more relevant risk factors that are less frequently discussed. These include poverty, education, discrimination, and home life.[8]
- Many sources of violent media content are satirical and not intended to be taken literally or as a valorization of violence. The problem is that many of these media products are also intended for adults or older audiences. Children don't generally develop the ability to recognize satire until around age 12.[9]
- We need to keep in mind that all children are not the same and what may disturb one child may have no effect at all on another. Moreover, development issues, emotional maturity, and relationships with peers and family seem to play a much more significant role in determining if a child is at risk for violent behaviour.[10]

A number of older studies and the criticisms about them remain relevant today as well. Ever since the 1950s, laboratory experiments have consistently shown that exposure to violence is associated with increased heartbeat, blood pressure and respiration rate, and a greater willingness to inflict pain or punishment on others. However, this line of enquiry has been criticized because of its focus on short term results and the artificial nature of the viewing environment.

A number of surveys indicate that children and young people who report a preference for violent entertainment also score higher on aggression indexes than those who watch less violent shows. L. Rowell Huesmann reviewed studies conducted in Australia, Finland, Poland, Israel, Netherlands and the United States and reported that "the child most likely to be aggressive would be the one who (a) watches violent television programs most of the time, (b) believes that these shows portray life just as it is, [and] (c) identifies strongly with the aggressive characters in the shows."[11] However, it may equally be that youth with tendencies towards violence are more likely to enjoy violent media.

In a study conducted by the Kaiser Family Foundation in 2003[12] nearly half (47 per cent) of parents with children between the ages of four and six reported that their children had imitated aggressive behaviours from TV. However, it is interesting to note that children are more likely to mimic positive behaviours — 87 per cent of kids do so.

Kansas State University professor John Murray[13] concluded in his research that "the most plausible interpretation of this pattern of correlations is that early preference for violent television programming and other media is one factor in the production of aggressive and antisocial behavior when the young boy becomes a young man."

A number of studies have reported that watching media violence frightens young children,[14] and that the effects of this may be long lasting.

In 1998, Professors Singer, Slovak, Frierson and York[15] surveyed 2,000 Ohio students in Grades three through eight. They reported that the incidences of psychological trauma (including anxiety, depression and post-traumatic stress) increased in proportion to the number of hours of television watched each day.

A 1999 survey of 500 Rhode Island parents led by Brown University professor Judith Owens[16] revealed that the presence of a television in a child's bedroom made it more likely that the child would suffer from sleep disturbances. Nine per cent of all the parents surveyed reported that their children had nightmares because of a television show at least once a week.

Tom Van der Voort[17] studied 314 children ages nine through 12 in 1986. He found that although children can easily distinguish cartoons, westerns and spy thrillers from reality, they often confuse realistic programs with the real world. When they are unable to integrate the violence in these shows because they can't follow the plot, they are much more likely to become anxious. This is particularly problematic because the children reported that they prefer realistic programs, which they equate with fun and excitement. Similar studies[18, 19] have since been conducted in the 90s with results corroborating Van der Voort's findings. As Jacques de Guise[20] reported in 2002, the younger the child, the less likely he or she will be able to identify violent content as violence.

In 1994, researchers Fred Molitor and Ken Hirsch[21] found that children are more likely to tolerate aggressive behaviour in the real world if they first watch TV shows or films that contain violent content.

George Gerbner conducted the longest running study of television violence. His seminal research suggests that heavy TV viewers tend to perceive the world in ways that are consistent with the images on TV. As viewers' perceptions of the world come to conform with the depictions they see on TV, they become more passive, more anxious, and more fearful. Gerbner called this the "Mean World Syndrome."[22]

Gerbner's research found that those who watch greater amounts of television are more likely to:

- overestimate their risk of being victimized by crime
- believe their neighbourhoods are unsafe
- believe "fear of crime is a very serious personal problem"
- assume the crime rate is increasing, even when it is not

André Gosselin, Jacques de Guise and Guy Paquette decided to test Gerbner's theory in the Canadian context in 1997.[23] They surveyed 360 university students, and found that heavy television viewers are more likely to believe the world is a more dangerous place. However, they also found heavy viewers are not actually more likely to be more afraid.

A number of studies since then suggest that media is only one of a number of variables that put children at risk of aggressive behaviour. For example, a Norwegian study[24] that included 20 at-risk teenaged boys found that the lack of parental rules regulating what the boys watched was a more significant predictor of aggressive behaviour than the amount of media violence they watched. It also indicated that exposure to real world violence, together with exposure to media violence, created an "overload" of violent events. Boys who experienced this overload were more likely to use violent media images to create and consolidate their identities as members of an anti-social and marginalized group.

On the other hand, researchers report that parental attitudes towards media violence can mitigate the impact it has on children. Huesmann and Bacharach conclude, "Family attitudes and social class are stronger determinants of attitudes toward aggression than is the amount of exposure to TV, which is nevertheless a significant but weaker predictor."

What should be apparent to us when we look at these kinds of claims and studies is that media violence is a highly complex and nuanced issue. There are clearly concerns with regards to violent media content such as age-appropriateness, saturation, desensitization, and instilling fear or unease in viewers. At the same time, many of the media products through which we are exposed to violent imagery provide benefits as well. Games and movies may expose young people to some violent content, but studies increasingly show that they also offer positive benefits. There is no way to completely shut out violent content, or to guarantee that children will never play video games that are rated as too old for them, or to make certain that everyone's feelings on what is inappropriate content will coincide with industry self-regulation practices. What concerned adults and parents can do, however, is promote critical engagement with the media that young people and children consume, monitor their children's media use, and discuss and establish rules at home to let young people understand what is or is not appropriate. More on how to talk about media violence with children can be found in the subsection Critically Engaging with Media Violence. If you are interested in legislation and industry tools that can help you to understand laws or give you a better idea of what to look out for, see our Government and Industry Responses to Media Violence (http://mediasmarts.ca/violence/government-and-industry-responses-media-violence).

Endnotes

1. "The School Shooting/Violent Videogame Link: Causal Relationship or Moral Panic?" *Journal of Investigative Psychology and Offender Profiling* Volume 5, Issue 1-2, Article first published online: 9 DEC 2008. (http://onlinelibrary.wiley.com/doi/10.1002/jip.76/pdf)

2. "A longitudinal test of video game violence influences on dating and aggression: A 3-year longitudinal study of adolescents." Ferguson, Christopher J., et. Al. *Journal of Psychiatric Research.* Volume 46, Issue 2 , Pages 141-146, February 2012. (http://www.journalofpsychiatricresearch.com/article/PIIS0022395611002627/abstract)

3. "Understanding the Effects of Violent Video Games on Violent Crime." Cunningham, Scott. Benjamin Engelstätter and Michael R. Ward. April 7, 2011. (http://papers.ssrn.com/sol3/papers.cfm?abstract_id=1804959)

4. "The Relationship Between Selective Exposure and the Enjoyment of Television Violence." Andrew J. Weaver, Matthew J. Kobach. *Aggressive Behaviour* Vol. 8 14 FEB 2012. (http://onlinelibrary.wiley.com/doi/10.1002/ab.2012.38.issue-2/issuetoc)

5. "Does excessive play of violent first-person-shooter-video-games dampen brain activity in response to emotional stimuli?" *Biological Psychology*, Jan. 2012. (http://www.ncbi.nlm.nih.gov/pubmed/21982747)

6. "Violent Entertainment Pitched to Adolescents: An Analysis of PG-13 Films". Theresa Webb, Lucille Jenkins, Nickolas Browne, Abdelmonen A. Afifi, and Jess Kraus. *Pediatrics* June 2007. (http://pediatrics.aappublications.org/content/119/6/e1219.full)

7. "Longitudinal Effects of Violent Video Games on Aggression in Japan and the United States". Craig A. Anderson, Akira Sakamoto, Douglas A. Gentile, Nobuko Ihori, Akiko Shibuya, Shintaro Yukawa, Mayumi Naito, and Kumiko Kobayashi. *Pediatrics* November 2008. (http://pediatrics.aappublications.org/content/122/5.toc)

8. "The Roots of Youth Violence": Government of Ontario. 2008. (http://www.children.gov.on.ca/htdocs/English/topics/youthandthelaw/roots/index.aspx)

9. Dr. Lawrence Steinberg, Developmental Psychologist. Temple University. Qtd. In: *Grand Theft Childhood*. Kutner, Lawrence and Cheryl K. Olson. Simon & Shuster, NY, 2008.

10. *Grand Theft Childhood*: Kutner, Lawrence and Cheryl K. Olson. Simon & Shuster, NY, 2008.

11. Huesmann, L.R. Television and Aggressive Behaviour. Television and Behaviour: Ten Years of Scientific Progress and Implications for the Eighties. Institute of Mental Health. Rockville, MD. 1982

12. Rideout, V et al. *Zero to Six*. Kaiser Family Foundation. 2003

13. Murray, John. *The Impact of Televised Violence*. Hofstra Law Review V. 22. 1994

14. Owens, J., Maxim, R., McGuinn, M., Nobile, C., Msall, M., & Alario, A. (1999). Television-viewing habits and sleep disturbance in school children. *Pediatrics*, 104 (3), 552.

15. Singer, Mi. et al. *Viewing Preferences, Symptoms of Psychological Trauma, and Violent Behaviours Among Children Who Watch Television*. Journal of American Academic Child and Adolescent Psychiatry. 1998.

16. Owens J, Maxim R, Nobile C, McGuinn M, Alario A, Msall M. *Television viewing habits and sleep disturbances in school-aged children*. Pediatrics, 1999;104(3):e 27

17. Van der Voort, T.H. *Television Violence: A Child's Eye View*. Amsterdam. Elsevier, 1986.

18. Wright, John C. et al. *Young Children's Perceptions of Television Reality*. Developmental Psychology, VOl. 30. 1994.

19. Chandler, Daniel. *Children's Understanding of What is Real on Television*. 1997

20. DeGuise, Jacques. *Analyse des émissions de fiction diffusées par les six réseaux généralistes*, 2002.

21. Molitor, Fred, & Hirsch, Kenneth W. (1994). *Children's toleration of real-life aggression after exposure to media violence: A replication of the Drabman and Thomas studies*. Child Study Journal, 24(3)

22. Gerbner, G. *Violence and Terror in the Mass Media.* Reports and Paper on Mass Communication No. 102). France: UNESCO.

23. Gosselin, A. et al. *Violence on Canadian Television and Some of Its Cognitive Effects.* Canadian Journal of Communication. Vol. 22, No2. 1997

24. Karlsen, Faltin and Trine Syvertsen. *Media Regulation and Parents.* Statens Filmtilsyn. 2004

> *"We need to know more about how to support children directly affected by bullying, and more work is needed in developing effective interventions for cyberbullying."*

Cyberbullying Cannot Be Ignored

Andrew Przybylski

In the following viewpoint, Andrew Przybylski argues that the modern-day problem of cyberbullying is not going away. In fact, the problem is growing, and it must be addressed despite its continued status as less prevalent than in-person physical and emotional bullying. The viewpoint gathers views of two Oxford experts who embarked on wide-ranging studies of cyberbullying among British young people to conclude that cyberbullying is a problem that should be addressed. How to address it, however, is another question. Andrew Przbylski is an experimental psychologist and Associate Professor, Senior Research Fellow and Director of Research, Oxford Internet Institute, part of the University of Oxford.

As you read, consider the following questions:

1. Is cyberbullying different in England than in the United States, according to the viewpoint?
2. How does cyberbullying impact victims as compared to in-person emotional bullying?
3. Is cyberbullying among adults less dangerous and impactful than cyberbullying among young people?

Bullying is a major public health problem, with systematic reviews supporting an association between adolescent bullying and poor mental wellbeing outcomes. In their Lancet article "Cyberbullying and adolescent well-being in England: a population-based cross sectional study," Andrew Przybylski (Oxford Internet Institute) and Lucy Bowes (Oxford's Dept of Experimental Psychology) report the largest study to date on the prevalence of traditional and cyberbullying, based on a nationally representative sample of 120,115 adolescents in England.

While nearly a third of the adolescent respondents reported experiencing significant bullying in the past few months, cyberbullying was much less common, with around five percent of respondents reporting recent significant experiences. Both traditional and cyberbullying were independently associated with lower mental well-being, but only the relation between traditional bullying and well-being was robust. This supports the view that cyberbullying is unlikely to provide a source for new victims, but rather presents an avenue for further victimisation of those already suffering from traditional forms of bullying.

This stands in stark contrast to media reports and the popular perception that young people are now more likely to be victims of cyberbullying than traditional forms. The results also suggest that interventions to address cyberbullying will only be effective if they also consider the dynamics of traditional forms of bullying, supporting the urgent need for evidence-based interventions that target *both* forms of bullying in adolescence.

That said, as social media and Internet connectivity become an increasingly intrinsic part of modern childhood, initiatives fostering resilience in online and every day contexts will be required.

We caught up with Andy and Lucy to discuss their findings:

Ed.: You say that given "the rise in the use of mobile and online technologies among young people, an up to date estimation of the current prevalence of cyberbullying in the UK is needed." Having undertaken that—what are your initial thoughts on the results?

Andy: I think a really compelling thing we learned in this project is that researchers and policymakers have to think very carefully about what constitutes a meaningful degree of bullying or cyberbullying. Many of the studies and reports we reviewed were really loose on details here while a smaller core of work was precise and informative. When we started our study it was difficult to sort through the noise but we settled on a solid standard—at least two or three experiences of bullying in the past month—to base our prevalence numbers and statistical models on.

Lucy: One of the issues here is that studies often use different measures, so it is hard to compare like for like, but in general our study supports other recent studies indicating that relatively few adolescents report being cyberbullied only—one study by Dieter Wolke and colleagues that collected between 2014–2015 found that whilst 29% of school students reported being bullied, only 1% of 11–16 year olds reported only cyberbullying. Whilst that study was only in a handful of schools in one part of England, the findings are strikingly similar to our own. In general then it seems that rates of cyberbullying are not increasing dramatically; though it is concerning that prevalence rates of both forms of bullying—particularly traditional bullying—have remained unacceptably high.

Ed.: Is there a policy distinction drawn between "bullying" (i.e. young people) and "harassment" (i.e. the rest of us, including in the workplace)—and also between "bullying" and "cyber-bullying"? These are all basically the same thing, aren't they—why distinguish?

Lucy: I think this is a good point; people do refer to 'bullying' in the workplace as well. Bullying, at its core, is defined as intentional, repeated aggression targeted against a person who is less able to defend him or herself—for example, a younger or more vulnerable person. Cyberbullying has the additional definition of occurring only in an online format—but I agree that this is the same action or behaviour, just taking place in a different context. Whilst in practice bullying and harassment have very similar meanings and may be used interchangeably, harassment is unlawful under the Equality Act 2010, whilst bullying actually isn't a legal term at all. However certain acts of bullying could be considered harassment and therefore be prosecuted. I think this really just reflects the fact that we often 'carve up' human behaviour and experience according to our different policies, practices and research fields—when in reality they are not so distinct.

Ed.: I suppose online bullying of young people might be more difficult to deal with, given it can occur under the radar, and in social spaces that might not easily admit adults (though conversely, leave actual evidence, if reported). Why do you think there's a moral panic about cyberbullying—is it just newspapers selling copy, or does it say something interesting about the Internet as a medium—a space that's both very open and very closed? And does any of this hysteria affect actual policy?

Andy: I think our concern arises from the uncertainty and unfamiliarity people have about the possibilities the Internet provides. Because it is full of potential—for good and ill—and is always changing, wild claims about it capture our imagination and fears. That said, the panic absolutely does affect policy and parenting discussions in the UK. Statistics and figures coming from pressure groups and well-meaning charities do put the prevalence of cyberbullying at terrifying, and unrealistically high, levels. This certainly has affected the way parents see things. Policy makers tend to seize on the worse case scenario and interpret things through this lens. Unfortunately this can be a distraction when there are known health and behavioural challenges facing young people.

Lucy: For me, I think we do tend to panic and highlight the negative impacts of the online world—often at the expense of the many positive impacts. That said, there was—and remains—a worry that cyberbullying could have the potential to be more widespread, and to be more difficult to resolve. The perpetrator's identity may be unknown, may follow the child home from school, and may be persistent—in that it may be difficult to remove hurtful comments or photos from the Internet. It is reassuring that our findings, as well as others', suggest that cyberbullying may not be associated with as great an impact on well-being as people have suggested.

Ed.: Obviously something as deeply complex and social as bullying requires a complex, multivalent response: but (that said), do you think there are any low-hanging interventions that might help address online bullying, like age verification, reporting tools, more information in online spaces about available help, more discussion of it as a problem (etc.)?

Andy: No easy ones. Understanding that cyber- and traditional bullying aren't dissimilar, parental engagement and keeping lines of communication open are key. This means parents should learn about the technology their young people are using, and that kids should know they're safe disclosing when something scary or distressing eventually happens.

Lucy: Bullying is certainly complex; school-based interventions that have been successful in reducing more traditional forms of bullying have tended to involve those students who are not directly involved but who act as "bystanders"—encouraging them to take a more active stance against bullying rather than remaining silent and implicitly suggesting that it is acceptable. There are online equivalents being developed, and greater education that discourages people (both children and adults) from sharing negative images or words, or encourages them to actively "dislike" such negative posts show promise. I also think it's important that targeted advice and support for those directly affected is provided.

Ed.: Who's seen as the primary body responsible for dealing with bullying online: is it schools? NGOs? Or the platform owners who actually (if not-intentionally) host this abuse? And does this topic bump up against wider current concerns about (e.g.) the moral responsibilities of social media companies?

Andy: There is no single body that takes responsibility for this for young people. Some charities and government agencies, like the Child Exploitation and Online Protection command (CEOP) are doing great work. They provide a forum for information for parents and professionals for kids that is stratified by age, and easy-to-complete forms that young people or carers can use to get help. Most industry-based solutions require users to report and flag offensive content and they're pretty far behind the ball on this because we don't know what works and what doesn't. At present cyberbullying consultants occupy the space and the services they provide are of dubious empirical value. If industry and the government want to improve things on this front they need to make direct investments in supporting robust, open, basic scientific research into cyberbulling and trials of promising intervention approaches.

Lucy: There was an interesting discussion by the NSPCC about this recently, and it seems that people are very mixed in their opinions— some would also say parents play an important role, as well as

Government. I think this reflects the fact that cyberbullying is a complex social issue. It is important that social media companies are aware, and work with government, NGOs and young people to safeguard against harm (as many are doing), but equally schools and parents play an important role in educating children about cyberbullying—how to stay safe, how to play an active role in reducing cyberbullying, and who to turn to if children are experiencing cyberbullying.

Ed.: You mention various limitations to the study; what further evidence do you think we need, in order to more completely understand this issue, and support good interventions?

Lucy: I think we need to know more about how to support children directly affected by bullying, and more work is needed in developing effective interventions for cyberbullying. There are some very good school-based interventions with a strong evidence base to suggest that they reduce the prevalence of at least traditional forms of bullying, but they are not being widely implemented in the UK, and this is a missed opportunity.

Andy: I agree—a focus on flashy cyberbullying headlines presents the real risk of distracting us from developing and implementing evidence-based interventions. The Internet cannot be turned off and there are no simple solutions.

Ed.: You say the UK is ranked 20th of 27 EU countries on the mental well-being index, and also note the link between well-being and productivity. Do you think there's enough discussion and effort being put into well-being, generally? And is there even a general public understanding of what "well-being" encompasses?

Lucy: I think the public understanding of well-being is probably pretty close to the research definition—people have a good sense that this involves more than not having psychological difficulty for example, and that it refers to friendships, relationships, and doing well; one's overall quality of life. Both research and policy is placing more of an emphasis on well-being—in part because large international studies have suggested that the UK may score particularly poorly on measures of well-being. This is very important if we are going to raise standards and improve people's quality of life.

> *"While most mentally ill individuals are not and never will become violent, certain types of serious mental illness—especially when untreated—are associated with a higher prevalence of certain types of firearm-related violence."*

Mental Illness Plays a Huge Role in Gun Violence

Amy Swearer

In the following viewpoint, Amy Swearer argues that mental illness plays the most significant role in the proliferation of mass shootings and other forms of gun violence. The author further offers that other explanations for the phenomenon and legal pushes to solve the problem miss the mark. Swearer does not believe that mentally ill people in general constitute a threat. But she does feel there is sufficient proof that those who have committed such heinous acts have proven to suffer from mental issues that could have been addressed to prevent tragedy. Amy Swearer is a legal policy analyst in the Meese Center for Legal and Judicial Studies.

"The Role of Mental Illness in Mass Shootings, Suicides," by Amy Swearer, The Heritage Foundation, February 12, 2019. Reprinted by permission.

As you read, consider the following questions:

1. How does the viewpoint's source, the Heritage Foundation, lean regarding gun issues?
2. Do you feel that enough people have a strong enough read on the mental health of potential shooters to prevent such events from happening?
3. How does the author indicate that guns are not the problem when it comes to mass shootings?

This week marks the one-year anniversary of the horrific Parkland school shooting. That tragedy sparked an intense national debate over how best to protect our children from school shootings.

Some have pushed for more restrictions on the constitutional rights of law-abiding citizens. Among them are the American Federation of Teachers and the National Education Association. These groups released a new set of proposals on Monday that they say "can prevent mass shooting incidents and help end gun violence in American schools."

Unfortunately, these proposals miss the mark by neglecting to focus on the real problems, including, among other things, the role of mental illness in certain types of firearm-related violence.

How does serious mental illness factor in? And what steps can government take to mitigate the role of untreated mental illness in producing violent threats?

These questions merit deliberate, thoughtful examination, not reflexive calls for broad gun control.

For that reason, The Heritage Foundation recently published a legal memorandum, "Mental Illness, Firearms, and Violence," as part of a series of papers by John Malcolm and myself exploring some of these deeper issues.

The paper makes clear that, while most mentally ill individuals are not and never will become violent, certain types of serious mental illness—especially when untreated—are associated with a higher prevalence of certain types of firearm-related violence.

In particular, individuals with serious mental illness are at a greater risk of committing suicide and are responsible for a disproportionate number of mass public killings.

Mass Public Shootings

There's no evidence that all mentally ill people constitute a "high risk" population with respect to interpersonal violence, including firearm-related violence against others.

In fact, most studies indicate that mental illness is responsible for only a small fraction (about 3 percent to 5 percent) of all violent crimes committed in the United States every year, and most of those episodes of violence are committed by individuals who are not currently receiving mental health treatment.

There is, however, a strong connection between acts of mass public violence—including mass public shootings—and untreated serious mental illness.

While acts of mass public violence are extraordinary and rare occurrences, they are often high-profile events that deeply affect the national view of violent crime trends. Mass public shootings in particular stoke national conversations on gun violence and gun control, for understandable reasons.

The majority of all mass public killers (some studies estimate as many as two-thirds) likely suffered from a serious mental illness prior to their attacks, and often displayed clear signs of delusional thinking, paranoia, or irrational feelings of oppression associated with conditions such as schizophrenia and bipolar-related psychosis.

This includes many individuals who committed atrocious attacks on students, including the Parkland shooter, the Virginia Tech shooter, and the Sandy Hook shooter—all of whom had long histories of untreated mental health problems.

Unfortunately, hardly any of these individuals were receiving psychiatric treatment at the time of their attacks.

Even without access to firearms, individuals with untreated serious mental illness can and do find ways to commit mass public killings.

Activist groups and politicians who point to mass public shootings as a reason for broad restrictions on firearm access by the general public largely miss the underlying reality: The real problem is not the prevalence of firearms among the general public, but the prevalence of untreated serious mental illness that causes some individuals to become violent in catastrophic ways, regardless of lawful access to firearms.

Suicide

The most significant link between mental illness and firearm-related violence is suicide, which accounts for almost two-thirds of all annual firearm-related deaths in the United States.

Of course, not every suicide is necessarily related to an underlying mental illness, but there is little doubt that the presence of a mental illness substantially increases a person's risk for committing suicide.

The most common method of suicide in the US is through the use of a firearm, an unsurprising reality given that the US has the highest per-capita number of privately owned firearms in the world.

Despite the nation's exceptionally high rate of suicide by firearm, however, it does not have a particularly high overall suicide rate, compared with other countries.

Our national suicide rate stands at roughly the world average and is comparable to the rate experienced by many European countries with significantly lower rates of private firearm ownership.

At the same time, a number of countries with severely restrictive gun control laws have much higher rates of suicide than the United States, including Belgium, Finland, France, Japan, and South Korea.

The connection between general measures of firearm access and general suicide rates is limited, at best. The US suicide rate has remained relatively stable over the past 50 years, even though the number of guns per capita has doubled.

Moreover, the percentage of suicides committed with firearms has actually decreased since 1999, even though the number of privately owned firearms has increased by more than 100 million.

As this data suggests, broad restrictions on firearm access are unlikely to have a meaningful effect on general suicide rates, and there are other socioeconomic factors beyond firearm availability that better account for differences in suicide rates.

These factors largely include measures of "social cohesion," such as divorce rates, unemployment, poverty, past trauma, and family structure, and it's increasingly clear that more socially integrated communities also tend to have lower suicide rates.

Access to firearms may, however, exacerbate the danger for people who are already at a heightened risk for committing suicide. For example, when individuals have a serious mental illness, access to firearms appears to increase their risk of committing suicide.

But it's also more complicated: While individuals with serious mental illness may have an increased risk of committing suicide when they have ready access to firearms, they may also be less likely than the general population to commit suicide with firearms.

Why? Because they often have greater barriers to legal firearm access, including disqualifying mental health histories under state or federal law, and concerned friends or family members who may limit their unsupervised access to firearms.

Several studies suggest, then, that reducing unsupervised access to all commonly employed means of suicide (including firearms, but also sharp objects, medications, and rope material) for at-risk persons reduces their individual risk of suicide.

In short, broad limitations on firearm access for individuals who are not necessarily at heightened risk for committing suicide are unlikely to meaningfully affect overall suicide rates and should be viewed with a heavy dose of skepticism, but policies designed to limit firearm access for individuals with serious mental illness may be an important step in the right direction for reducing state and national suicide rates.

Policy Implications

It is clear that mental illness—especially untreated serious mental illness—plays a significant role in certain types of firearm-related violence that cannot be ignored.

This is not to suggest that individuals with mental illness should be treated as community pariahs or that they are even the cause of most firearm-related violence in the United States. But any holistic approach to reducing suicide and violent crime rates in our communities must account for the role played by serious mental illness.

The reduction of suicide rates requires a comprehensive approach that addresses all of the various factors related to suicide risk, including mental illness, socioeconomic variations, and access to a support system.

Similarly, policies to reduce the rate of mass public shootings in the United States must account for the significant role played by untreated serious mental illness in such killings.

The broad-scale disarmament of the general population is an inappropriate and unnecessary substitute for dealing with the underlying problems.

> "*Blaming mental illness for the gun violence in our country is simplistic and inaccurate and goes against the scientific evidence currently available.*"

Blaming Mass Shootings on Mental Illness Leads to Stigma

Jessica Glenza

In the following viewpoint, Jessica Glenza argues that blaming gun violence on mental illness can have dangerous consequences. The author uses President Trump's address following a mass shooting to emphasize the danger in his assignation of blame on mental illness. She quotes psychology experts, who insist that the majority of mentally ill people are neither violent nor dangerous, to debunk Trump's theories. Blaming mass shootings on mental health does not help those who suffer from mental illness, and indeed the government has made no real strides in addressing the issue of mental health treatment. Jessica Glenza is the health reporter for Guardian US.

"Blaming Mass Shootings on Mental Illness Leads to Stigma, Experts Warn," by Jessica Glenza, Guardian News and Media Limited, August 6, 2019. Reprinted by permission.

As you read, consider the following questions:

1. What did mental health experts blame for mass shootings as they condemned Trump's statements?
2. What is the only country with a higher rate of mass shootings than the United States?
3. What is one example of the government reducing mental health care, according to the viewpoint?

Blaming gun violence on the mentally ill prevents America from solving its unique gun violence problem, and stigmatizes those with diagnoses, psychologists and psychiatrists warned following the El Paso and Dayton mass shootings.

Experts in mental health have repeated these lines for decades since the deadly school shooting at Columbine High School in Colorado, and made statements again Monday, after Donald Trump blamed mental illness for two back-to-back shootings in El Paso, Texas, and Dayton, Ohio, that left 31 people dead and dozens injured.

In an address to the nation, Trump said: "Mental illness and hatred pulls the trigger, not the gun." He also called the gunman from Dayton, Ohio, a "twisted monster," and both shootings "evil attacks."

The leading associations of psychiatrists and psychologists both condemned the statement, while pointing to a defining characteristic of American life: easy access to guns.

"Blaming mental illness for the gun violence in our country is simplistic and inaccurate and goes against the scientific evidence currently available," said Arthur C Evans Jr, CEO of the American Psychological Association.

"As we psychological scientists have said repeatedly, the overwhelming majority of people with mental illness are not violent," said Evans. "And there is no single personality profile that can reliably predict who will resort to gun violence.

"Based on the research, we know only that a history of violence is the single best predictor of who will commit future violence. And access to more guns, and deadlier guns, means more lives lost." Evans called on lawmakers to pass gun restrictions, including a limit on civilians' access to assault weapons and high capacity magazines.

The US has become home to 31% of all mass shootings globally, and is also home to half of all the 650m civilian-owned guns in the world, despite having just 5% of the population, according to an analysis by Adam Lankford, criminology professor at the University of Alabama. In a comparison of 171 countries with more than 10 million people, only Yemen has a higher rate of mass shootings. It is ranked second in terms of firearms ownership per resident.

In the same analysis, rates of homicide and suicide rates varied among the 171 counties, indicating a lack of correlation between mental illness and firearms homicides.

Trump also asserted video games may be responsible for firearms deaths. However, Americans play at similar or even lower rates compared to other industrialized nations, failing to explain America's extraordinarily high rate of mass shootings.

In his speech Monday, Trump also called for "involuntary confinement" of "mentally disturbed individuals"—it is unclear what he means by this. While mental illness does not explain the high incidence of mass shootings in America, experts largely agree America's mental healthcare infrastructure is broken.

Beginning roughly in the 1960s, the movement to "deinstitutionalize" patients from state hospitals pushed the mentally ill into pharmaceutical, out-patient-based therapies.

It also resulted in a 95% decline in the number of long-term psychiatric beds available in the US, and a movement of the mentally ill from state-run hospitals to jails, emergency departments and homelessness. According to 2006 data from the Bureau of Justice Statistics, 55% of male and 73% of female inmates in state jails have a mental health problem.

5 Things You Can Do to Stop Gun Violence

Since 1988, the Violence Policy Center has worked to stop gun death and injury through research, education, advocacy, and collaboration. The VPC informs the public about the impact of gun violence on their daily lives, exposes the profit-driven marketing and lobbying activities of the firearms industry and gun lobby, offers unique technical expertise to policymakers, organizations, and advocates on the federal, state, and local levels, and works for policy changes that save lives.

The VPC has a long and proven record of policy successes on the federal, state, and local levels, leading the National Rifle Association to acknowledge the Center as "the most effective ... anti-gun rabble rouser in Washington."

Here are five things you can do right now to help stop gun violence.

1. Contact your elected representatives and demand that they support and advocate for effective gun violence prevention legislation. Call your US Senators and Representative via the US Capitol Switchboard at 202-224-3121 and tell them that you

Some psychiatrists, such as professor Dominic Sisti of the University of Pennsylvania, have called on governments to reintroduce public support for long-term psychiatric care.

"Asylums are a necessary but not sufficient component of a reformed spectrum of psychiatric services," Sisti wrote in an editorial for the Journal of the American Medical Association. "A return to asylum-based long-term psychiatric care will not remedy the complex problems of the US mental health system, especially for patients with milder forms of mental illness who can thrive with high-quality outpatient care.

"Reforms that ignore the importance of expanding the role of such institutions will fail mental health patients who cannot live

SUPPORT a federal ban on assault weapons and high-capacity ammunition magazines.

2. Make an online tax-deductible contribution to the Violence Policy Center.

Or, engage your friends to take a stand against gun violence. Create your very own online fundraiser in just 10 minutes. Visit the Violence Policy Center's pages on the crowdfunding sites Crowdrise and Mightycause.

3. Join a local gun violence prevention organization. Visit States United to Prevent Gun Violence, the national umbrella organization for state gun violence prevention organizations to find a group in your state.

4. Write a letter to the editor in your local paper in support of gun violence prevention. Or use social media to support the Violence Policy Center's efforts to stop gun violence. Visit the Center's Twitter feed or our Facebook page for tweets and postings detailing the facts about gun violence, as well as effective solutions.

5. Host your very own evening of information and action to educate your friends and community about gun violence while helping support the Violence Policy Center.

"5 Things You Can Do Now to Stop Gun Violence," Violence Policy Center.

alone, cannot care for themselves, or are a danger to themselves and others," Sisti wrote.

Republicans attempted, and failed, to further defund treatment for mental health by repealing the Affordable Care Act, better known as Obamacare. Obamacare expanded Medicaid, a health insurance program for the poor and disabled. Medicaid is responsible for one quarter of the nation's mental health spending, according to the National Council for Behavioral Health. The program provides healthcare for 74 million Americans.

Republicans, including Ohio's governor, this week have also called for "red flag laws" in response to the mass shootings, which have been passed in 17 states. These allow police to temporarily take custody of a person's firearms if they are believed to be a risk to themselves or others, typically during a period of crisis. For example, a spouse could call the police and ask guns for a person's firearms to be temporarily confiscated because of increasing threats. Then, a court would hear the case.

An American Psychiatric Association working group examined the laws in 2018, after Trump proposed enacting them at a federal level. There is limited data on their utility at preventing violence —just Connecticut and Indiana have reported data – but there is some evidence they can prevent suicide. The working group called for more research into other violence prevention.

In Connecticut, most people whose guns were confiscated were middle-aged married men, who had no prior history of mental illness and were not involved with the criminal justice system. An average of seven guns were seized per warrant.

Periodical and Internet Sources Bibliography

The following articles have been selected to supplement the diverse views presented in this chapter.

American Psychological Association, "Violence in the Media." https://www.apa.org/action/resources/research-in-action/protect.

Art Bamford, "What Is the Real Impact of Violent Video Games?" Fuller Youth Institute. https://fulleryouthinstitute.org/blog/the-real-impact-of-violent-video-games.

Rhitu Chattterjee, "School Shooters: What's Their Path to Violence?" National Public Radio, February 10, 2019. https://www.npr.org/sections/health-shots/2019/02/10/690372199/school-shooters-whats-their-path-to-violence.

Mehdi Hasan, "After El Paso, We Can No Longer Ignore Trump's Role in Inspiring Mass Shootings," The Intercept, August 4, 2019. https://theintercept.com/2019/08/04/el-paso-dayton-mass-shootings-donald-trump/.

Adam Isaak, "Psychologists See Violent Video Games Differently than the Rest of Us," CNBC, December 22, 2019. https://www.cnbc.com/2019/12/20/scientists-disagree-completely-on-the-impact-of-violent-video-games.html.

Olga Khazan, "Why Many Mass Shooters Are Loners," *The Atlantic*, August 5, 2019. https://www.theatlantic.com/health/archive/2019/08/el-paso-shooting-when-loneliness-leads-mass-murder/595498/.

Maayan Simckes, "Guns in America: The Worrying Relationship Between School-Bullying and Gun Violence," *Newsweek*, July 1, 2017. https://www.newsweek.com/bullied-victims-and-gun-violence-american-schools-worrying-relationship-629752.

Jane C. Timm, "Fact Check: Trump Suggests Video Games to Blame for Mass Shootings," NBC News, August 5, 2019. https://www.nbcnews.com/politics/donald-trump/fact-check-trump-suggests-video-games-blame-mass-shootings-n1039411.

WBUR, "How Is Bullying Linked to Violence in Society?" March 19, 2018. https://www.wbur.org/hereandnow/2018/03/19/bullying-violence-society.

Are Guns the Root of the Problem?

Chapter Preface

It has become perhaps the most heated debate in the United States over the last twenty years. Is the easy access to guns the most significant reason for the disturbing rise in mass shootings? Or are society and mental health primarily to blame? Or is it something else entirely?

Most Americans believe the answer lies somewhere in the middle. They feel that citizens must become more vigilant in sounding the alarm on others they fear could be dangerous, in hopes that they can avert a tragedy. But they also believe that gun ownership or unfettered ability to purchase weapons plays a huge role in allowing such tragedies to happen.

Many complain that they live in a gun culture. Americans own nearly half of all the guns in the world. But this has been the reality for decades. Millions of people in other countries that do not suffer from mass shooting issues own guns as well. The debate is whether the comparative calm in those nations is due to stringent gun control laws or to the overall culture of their societies.

Are Americans more prone to the kinds of mental illnesses that trigger a desire to pull a trigger? Or is the gun culture to blame? Does America abandon the mentally unwell? And are the country's gun laws weaker than they should be? These are things that many Americans think should be pursued, yet nothing has been accomplished.

Even if guns are the root cause and gun control is the solution, many worry that it is simply too late to enact any effective changes to gun acquisition and ownership. They argue that massive number of guns already on American streets will make it impossible to keep them from those that seek to use them with evil intent. Others claim that stringent background checks would solve that problem. But while the debate rages, innocent people continue to be gunned down.

> "Noticeably absent from the president's remarks was any mention of new restrictions on guns, despite the fact that just hours earlier Trump had urged the US Congress in a tweet to pass some form of background checks."

The President of the United States Is Blaming Everything but Guns for Mass Shootings

Sabrina Siddiqui

In the following viewpoint, Sabrina Siddiqui reacts to a speech given by President Donald Trump following two mass shootings in 2019. The author argues that any call for expanded background checks for gun purchases was conspicuously absent from Trump's rhetoric, despite the president's previous call for such checks. The author suggests that Trump, like many US politicians on the right, fears the reaction of the powerful National Rifle Association to any tact that would limit the availability of guns. The familiar refrain of "guns don't kill people, people kill people" continued to be heard after the tragedies. Trump's words worked to justify that point of view. Sabrina Siddiqui is a political reporter for the Guardian.

"Trump Blames 'Glorification of Violence' but Not Guns After Mass Shootings," by Sabrina Siddiqui, Guardian News and Media Limited, August 5, 2019. Reprinted by permission.

As you read, consider the following questions:

1. What claim does the author make as a reason why Congress has been unable to pass background checks on gun purchases?
2. Does the author betray any personal opinions in the viewpoint?
3. What role does President Trump claim the media plays in the spate of mass shootings, according to the viewpoint?

Donald Trump has blamed "the glorification of violence" in a speech that identified video games, the internet and mental illness—but not guns—as the cause of the slaughter that left at least 31 dead and 53 injured in less than 24 hours over the weekend.

In his first public remarks on the pair of shootings in El Paso, Texas, and Dayton, Ohio, Trump also condemned white supremacy as authorities said they were investigating an anti-Hispanic, anti-immigrant manifesto allegedly tied to the El Paso suspect.

"The shooter in El Paso posted a manifesto online consumed by racist hate," Trump said. "In one voice, our nation must condemn racism, bigotry and white supremacy."

"These sinister ideologies must be defeated. Hate has no place in America."

Noticeably absent from the president's remarks was any mention of new restrictions on guns, despite the fact that just hours earlier Trump had urged the US Congress in a tweet to pass some form of background checks.

Congress has proven unable to pass substantial gun violence legislation this session, despite the frequency of mass shootings, in large part because of resistance from Republicans, particularly in the Republican-controlled Senate. That political dynamic shows no signs of changing.

Shortly after Trump spoke, authorities said another person had died from injuries sustained during the mass shooting at a Walmart in El Paso on Saturday, raising the death toll in that attack to 22. El Paso police tweeted that the latest victim died early Monday morning at a hospital. No other details were immediately provided.

Speaking from the White House, Trump called for "real bipartisan solutions" but pointedly attempted to steer the dialogue away from firearms.

"Mental illness and hatred pulls the trigger, not the gun," Trump said, while calling for reforms that "better identify mentally disturbed individuals who may commit acts of violence."

He said authorities should "make sure those people not only get treatment, but, when necessary, involuntary confinement," but did not elaborate.

The president also said he was directing the justice department to draw up a proposal that would swiftly deliver the death penalty to those who commit hate crimes and mass murders, so that capital punishment could be rendered "quickly, decisively and without years of needless delay."

Trump further revived the widely debunked theory that video games were a factor in mass shootings, condemning "the gruesome and grisly video games that are now commonplace."

"It is too easy today for troubled youth to surround themselves with a culture that celebrates violence," he said. "We must stop or substantially reduce this, and it has to begin immediately."

The president's comments came hours after he suggested lawmakers in Washington link background checks legislation to "desperately needed immigration reform," drawing criticism for invoking immigration policy after one of the shootings targeted the predominantly Latino community of El Paso.

"Republicans and Democrats must come together and get strong background checks, perhaps marrying this legislation with desperately needed immigration reform," Trump tweeted. "We must have something good, if not GREAT, come out of these two tragic events!"

Trump also took aim at the media in his tweets, claiming "fake news" had played a role in the current climate.

"The Media has a big responsibility to life and safety in our Country," Trump wrote. "Fake News has contributed greatly to the anger and rage that has built up over many years.

"News coverage has got to start being fair, balanced and unbiased, or these terrible problems will only get worse!"

The mayor of El Paso confirmed that the president would be visiting the city on Wednesday.

Top Democrats swiftly condemned Trump's initial response to the shootings, with some drawing comparisons to Nazi Germany.

"What's [the] connection between background checks & immigration reform? That we have to keep guns out of the hands out of the invading hordes?" the House judiciary committee chairman, Jerry Nadler, said in an interview with MSNBC.

"That's disgusting. It reminds me of the 1930s in Germany."

The 2020 presidential candidate Beto O'Rourke, a native of El Paso, also likened Trump's comments to Nazi Germany: "The only modern western democracy that I can think of that said anything close to this is the Third Reich, Nazi Germany."

Another Democratic 2020 presidential candidate, Julián Castro, said: "Donald Trump is unfit to lead our nation. His words could not be more hollow. He says 'we must condemn racism, bigotry and white nationalism'—but often serves as their national spokesperson. In this national emergency, our president is morally bankrupt. We deserve better."

Twenty-one people were killed and another 26 injured in El Paso, which sits along the southern border and is heavily populated by immigrants. Authorities said at least six of the deceased were Mexican nationals.

The details of the El Paso shooting, at a popular shopping center on Saturday morning, were still being learned when another massacre unfolded overnight.

In a matter of 32 seconds, a gunman in Dayton, Ohio, killed nine and wounded at least 27 more on a busy street in the early hours of Sunday. The suspect, whose victims included his own sister, was killed by police when they arrived at the scene.

"Hate Has No Place in America"

Donald Trump vowed "to act with urgent resolve" on Monday morning following a weekend in which mass shootings in El Paso, Texas and Dayton, Ohio left 29 people dead.

"Our nation is overcome with shock, horror and sorrow," the president said during remarks at the Diplomatic Room of the White House.

"These barbaric slaughters are an assault upon our communities, an attack on our nation, and a crime against all of humanity," he added.

The gunman in El Paso is believed to be a white nationalist who authorities think may have posted a racist and anti-immigrant manifesto on the online message board 8chan shortly before opening fire on shoppers in a local Walmart. The gunman in Dayton has not been linked with any political ideology.

"In one voice our nation must condemn racism, bigotry and white supremacy," Trump said. "Hate has no place in America. Hatred warps the mind, ravages the heart, and devours the soul."

In the wake of the deadly attacks, Democrats faulted Trump for using divisive rhetoric that dehumanizes immigrants and people of color. Beto O'Rourke, a Democratic candidate for president who represented El Paso in Congress for six years, explicitly condemned the president.

The events kicked off an all-too-familiar debate over gun violence in America, which claims roughly 100 lives each day.

Trump has reneged on previous pledges to strengthen gun laws. After other mass shootings he called for strengthening the federal background check system, and in 2018 he signed legislation to increase federal agency data sharing into the system. But he has resisted Democratic calls to toughen other gun control laws.

In February, the House approved bipartisan legislation to require federal background checks for all gun sales and transfers

"He's not tolerating racism, he's promoting racism," O'Rourke said. "He's not tolerating violence, he's inciting racism and violence in this country."

At the same time, Trump is facing pressure to act from some members of his own party. Former Ohio Governor John Kasich said the federal government should consider instituting a "red flag law," which allow authorities to seize a person's firearms if they have social media posts indicating they are unstable, and the Rupert Murdoch owned New York Post, a conservative tabloid, urged President Trump to embrace an assault weapon ban. Other lawmakers had a different response, with Texas Lieutenant Governor Dan Patrick blaming violent video games and a lack of prayer in schools for the shootings.

In his remarks, Trump also placed blame on violent video games for inspiring killers and on the internet for providing a forum for hate speech. The president vowed to find bipartisan solutions to gun violence but did not offer many specifics about what actions should be taken.

The president suggested that tougher gun control laws such as more extensive background checks could be combined with "desperately needed immigration reform." But he also returned to a familiar punching bag, accusing the media of sowing discord.

"President Trump on Mass Shootings: 'Hate Has No Place in America,'" by Brent Lang, Variety Media, LLC, August 5, 2019.

and approved legislation to allow a review period of up to 10 days for background checks on firearms purchases. The White House threatened a presidential veto if those measures passed Congress.

At a February meeting with survivors and family members of the 2018 Parkland, Florida, school shooting in which 17 people died, Trump promised to be "very strong on background checks."

Trump claimed he would stand up to the gun lobby, but he later retreated, expressing support for modest changes to the federal background check system and for arming teachers.

On Monday, Trump's speech drew on ideas that Republicans in Congress can embrace without confronting the gun lobby or restricting access to weapons.

Kevin McCarthy, the House minority leader and a Trump ally, has raised concerns about violence in video games, while another Trump confidant, Senator Lindsey Graham, tweeted his support over the weekend for his own red flag mental health bill.

> *"There is public support for universal background checks for gun purchases, extreme risk protection orders (also called red flag laws), gun licensing, assault-weapons bans and bans on high-capacity magazines. But many of these issues are hotly polarizing."*

Americans Largely Support Gun Restrictions to "Do Something" About Gun Violence

Domenico Montanaro

In the following viewpoint, Domenico Montanaro addresses the call among Americans for their leaders to limit gun violence. Many frustrated and angry Americans have demanded that restrictions be placed on gun purchases, including background checks and an assault weapons ban. Even President Donald Trump called for implementation of stronger background checks, though the president later stepped back from that plan. The author charts the public's desires and the lack of action taken by the government since the turn of the century. Domenico Montanaro is a correspondent and senior political editor for National Public Radio (NPR).

As you read, consider the following questions:

1. What caused President Trump to recant his call for extensive background checks?
2. How does the author use statistics to prove that Americans want their leaders to "do something" about gun violence?
3. What are red flag laws?

After the mass shootings in Dayton, Ohio, and El Paso, Texas, gun control is again at the forefront of the political conversation.

President Trump has expressed openness to a federal red flag law and for "meaningful" background checks.

"Frankly, we need intelligent background checks," Trump told reporters Friday. He added, "On background checks, we have tremendous support for really common sense, sensible, important background checks."

What all that means exactly isn't clear yet. What is clear, from public opinion polling, is that Americans believe gun violence is a problem, and they support more restrictions on guns. That sentiment spilled over Sunday night when a frustrated crowd chanted "do something" at Ohio's Republican Gov. Mike DeWine following the mass shooting in Dayton. They eventually drowned out his attempt to roll out his plan to curb gun violence.

But momentum for gun restrictions has fallen apart in the past—stymied by groups like the National Rifle Association—and there doesn't yet appear to be a clear legislative strategy this time around. President Trump and Republicans will have a choice to make.

There is public support for universal background checks for gun purchases, extreme risk protection orders (also called red flag laws), gun licensing, assault-weapons bans and bans on high-capacity magazines. But many of these issues are hotly polarizing. While they mostly enjoy support from Democrats and independents, Republicans are not always on board.

Here's a look at where things stand, measure by measure, based on the latest polling and on Capitol Hill:

Americans Overall Support Stricter Gun Laws

A solid majority of Americans say they are in favor of stricter gun laws in the United States—61% said so in a May Quinnipiac poll. But the breakdown by party is illuminating—91% of Democrats think gun laws should be stricter, as do 59% of independents, but just 32% of Republicans.

Almost three-quarters (73%) in the poll also said more needs to be done to address gun violence.

A February NPR/PBS NewsHour/Marist poll found less support for stricter laws covering gun sales, but still a majority (51%) were in favor. Another 36% said the laws should be kept as they are.

But, like Quinnipiac, when people were asked if they thought it was more important to control gun violence or protect gun rights, 58% said control gun violence, the highest in at least six years. Just 37% responded that it was more important to protect gun rights.

Universal Background Checks

The president says he spoke with Senate Majority Leader Mitch McConnell, R-Ky., this week. Trump said McConnell is "totally on board" with background checks. Trump also spoke with House Speaker Nancy Pelosi and Senate Minority Leader Chuck Schumer, who want background checks passed together with red flag legislation.

McConnell said in an interview with a Kentucky radio station that any effort has to be bipartisan. On universal background checks, he acknowledged "there's a lot of support for that," that the issue will be "front and center, as we see what we can come together and pass."

According to the polls, there are few issues with as broad support as universal background checks—89% overall said they supported background checks for gun purchases at gun shows or other private sales, in a July NPR/PBS NewsHour/Marist poll.

Even 84% of Republicans are in favor of them, according to the poll. Another example: that May Quinnipiac poll had support for requiring background checks for all gun buyers at 94% overall (98% for Democrats, 94% independents, 92% Republicans).

It has been a similar story with most polling for years about universal background checks. The National Rifle Association, however, has been against them. Nothing has passed federally yet, but the president has said he would take the organization on.

But with the NRA facing internal financial problems and pro-gun-restrictions groups outspending it for the first time in the 2018 midterm elections, there's a question of whether Republicans are feeling the same kind of pressure from the group as in years past.

Red Flag Laws, or Extreme Risk Protection Orders

Some on Capitol Hill, like Republican Sens. Lindsey Graham of South Carolina and Marco Rubio of Florida, have already restarted a push for a federal red flag law.

These laws allow police to get what's known in many places as an extreme risk protection order and temporarily seize guns if someone reports seeing something that gives them concern that someone who owns a gun may be a risk to themselves or others.

More than a dozen states have passed varying forms of red flag laws, and they have been shown to be particularly effective at preventing suicides.

There has not been a lot of polling on red flag laws, but polling from some partisan outfits or funded by organizations that support these laws has found support for them.

One of the better national pollsters is the Democratic firm Hart Research (the Democratic half of the pollsters who conduct the NBC/Wall Street Journal poll). They polled on behalf of Everytown for Gun Safety, the gun restrictions advocacy group funded by former New York City Mayor Michael Bloomberg, who is no friend of the gun industry.

The poll of 1,200 likely voters before the 2018 midterm elections found that 89% wanted Congress to pass a red flag law, and 75% said they were more likely to support a candidate in favor of them.

An online poll conducted by YouGov Blue (a division of YouGov but serving Democratic and progressive clients) also found support for red flag laws, but to a lesser degree. The poll from April found 69% in favor of red flag laws, including 50% of Republicans.

It's a similar story on the state level. EPIC/MRA (a good polling outfit) in Michigan conducted a survey for the Michigan Chapter of the American Academy of Pediatrics and found that 70% were in favor of red flag laws. That included 78% of Democrats, 67% of independents and 64% of Republicans.

In Colorado, a Keating Research survey found 81% in favor of red flag laws, including 62% who were "strongly" in favor. By party, it was 92% of Democrats, 73% of Republicans and 79% of unaffiliated voters.

While there is generally Democratic support for such a law, Sen. Schumer, D-N.Y., wants red flag legislation married to universal background checks, because that has failed previously in the Senate—despite being widely popular.

Gun Licensing

Three-quarters (77%) said in the May Quinnipiac poll that they supported requiring individuals to obtain a license before being able to purchase a gun.

That included 65% of Republicans, so this is a popular idea, but there is little talk about it currently on Capitol Hill in response to the latest mass shootings.

Assault-Style Weapons Ban

A majority—57%—of Americans said they were in favor of a ban on the sale of semi-automatic assault guns such as the AK-47 or the AR-15, according to the July NPR poll. But while that's a solid majority, this is a very polarizing topic.

For example, 83% of Democrats said they were in favor of the ban, as were 55% of independents. But just 29% of Republicans said they thought it was a good idea. That's a whopping 54-point gap.

The Quinnipiac poll had support for a ban slightly higher, at 63%. It had GOP support 10 points higher at 39%, still a minority, and independents 8 points higher at 63%.

GUN CONTROL AND VIOLENT EXTREMISM

Easy access to powerful firearms is exposing America to attacks from violent extremists, an outgoing top counterterrorism official has warned.

"We find ourselves in a more dangerous situation because our population of violent extremists has no difficulty gaining access to weapons that are quite lethal," Nicholas Rasmussen of the National Counterterrorism Centre told the Washington Post. "I wish that weren't so."

High-profile mass shootings occur regularly in America, and assailants often wield legally obtained guns. In October, a gunman named Stephen Paddock killed more than 50 people and injured more than 500 after opening fire on a Las Vegas concert. It later emerged that he had been stockpiling firearms and ammunition which he was able to purchase after passing background checks.

In 2015, Syed Rizwan Farook and Tashfeen Malik opened fire on a San Bernardino, California regional centre with guns that were purchased legally from licensed firearms dealers—an associate who bought semiautomatic rifles and supplied them to the shooters later pleaded guilty to terrorism charges.

"More weapons, more readily available, increases the lethality of those that would pick them up and use them," added Mr Rasmussen, who served for three years as America's leading dedicated counter-terror official.

Assault-style weapons were banned in the 1990s during the Clinton presidency, and it's something that former President Bill Clinton has now come out and said he believes should be instituted again. But there's little appetite on Capitol Hill among Republicans for reinstating the ban.

High-Capacity Magazines

The February NPR poll also found two-thirds—65%—thought banning high-capacity ammunition clips would make a difference in reducing gun violence.

While such events typically spur a political debate about enacting tighter gun laws, the federal government has not imposed significant new firearms restrictions in years.

Federal law already prohibits people convicted of felonies and other crimes like domestic abuse from owning guns. A push to ban certain military-style rifles and impose broader background checks, championed by Barack Obama after 20 children and six adults died in a 2012 elementary school shooting, collapsed in Congress.

Gun control efforts tend to be more successful on the state and local level. After the Las Vegas shooting, for example, the city of Columbia, South Carolina, banned a device known as a "bump stock" that Paddock used to accelerate his rate of firing.

Of the tens of thousands of Americans who lose their lives to guns annually, only a sliver die in mass attacks. But the death rate from gun violence in general has risen in recent years.

According to the federal Centres for Disease Control, the frequency of firearm-related deaths grew for the second straight year in 2016 following a period of relative stability. About 12 deaths per 100,000 were attributable to firearms, which amounted to more than 38,000 fatalities.

"Easy Access to Guns Is Exposing US to Attacks from Violent Extremists, Warns Top Counterterrorism Official," by Jeremy B. White, The Independent, January 27, 2017.

While 86% of Democrats and 59% of independents said they thought it would make a difference, Republicans were split with 51% saying they didn't think it would make a difference.

That's been part of the conversation previously, notably with Democratic Sen. Dianne Feinstein of California after the Sandy Hook Elementary School shooting, but it went nowhere because of GOP and NRA opposition.

> "In terms of sweeping gun control, I haven't changed my view. And the reason for that is not that I don't care about what happened, or that I don't think it was a disaster for those involved, or that I wasn't personally affected, but because I just strongly disagree that gun control is the way you will stop this."

Gun Control Is Not the Solution

National Public Radio

In the following viewpoint, a transcript of an interview that aired on National Public Radio, Charles Cooke rails against what he perceives as the ineffectiveness of gun control in preventing school shootings. Cooke believes that the number of assault weapons and other guns available throughout the United States precludes the notion that gun control measures would make such weapons difficult for potential school shooters to procure them. He lambasts President Trump for what he believes to be a disjointed message on gun control and pushes back against any policies that would limit gun rights of law-abiding citizens. Charles Cooke is editor of National Review Online.

"Gun Control Is Not the Way to Stop School Shootings, Cooke Says," National Public Radio Inc. (NPR), March 2, 2018. Reprinted by permission.

As you read, consider the following questions:

1. Does Cooke make a valid point against gun control when he cites the number of weapons already available?
2. What stand does Cooke want President Trump to take on the gun control issue?
3. What does Cooke feel needs to be done about background checks?

Rachel Martin talks to Charles Cooke, *National Review Online* editor, about how the Florida shooting may have started a change of heart on gun policy in the White House, that sentiment isn't universal.

DAVID GREENE, HOST: And this week, President Trump pressed lawmakers to come up with a unified plan on gun policy that he can support.

(SOUNDBITE OF ARCHIVED RECORDING)

PRESIDENT DONALD TRUMP: We have to pursue commonsense measures that protect the rights of law-abiding Americans while keeping guns—and we have to keep the guns out of the hands of those that pose the threat.

GREENE: But it is not entirely clear what measures the president really supports. An NRA lobbyist met Trump yesterday and said that the president does not support gun control. Charles Cooke is editor of *National Review Online*. And while Cooke supports some regulations, he told Rachel Martin that the recent school shooting has not shaken his belief in gun rights.

CHARLES COOKE: We need to give law enforcement, as long as there is a due process component—a strong due process component —more leeway in removing guns from people who have shown themselves to be violent or have made threats. But in terms of sweeping gun control, I haven't changed my view. And the reason for that is not that I don't care about what happened, or that I don't think it was a disaster for those involved, or that I wasn't personally affected—I have children myself—but because I just strongly disagree that that is—that gun control is the way you will stop this.

RACHEL MARTIN, BYLINE: President Trump met with Democrats and Republicans from both House and Senate. And in that discussion about what to do about gun violence in the country, the president, a Republican, actually suggested that an assault weapons ban could be a good idea.

COOKE: Well, I think the president is entirely incoherent. He's also somebody who does not have particularly strong views in favor of guns. I understand that he has been defended by the NRA, both on his policy positions and also, oddly enough, just in general. But if you go back to Donald Trump 20 years ago, you will find somebody who was in favor of an assault weapons ban and waiting period and so forth. So we're dealing with an anomaly within the system.

I do think it is much more useful politically to look at the underlying political reality here. And that means looking at what Republicans think of this issue. And, you know, as much as Donald Trump flails around, I don't think that's going to change.

MARTIN: There have been other Republicans who have at least softened their language when thinking about an assault weapons ban. I interviewed a top Republican donor recently who said that he was going to stop supporting candidates who didn't fully embrace an assault weapons ban. Why do you argue that that's a bad idea?

COOKE: Well, I think it's a red herring. I don't think it will do anything. I mean, there are already 10 million AR-15s in the country. It's peculiar to me that we focus in on this weapon. It doesn't have a more lethal capacity than a handgun, especially in a close-range situation.

MARTIN: Do you support raising the age limit for someone to buy an assault-style weapon from 18 to 21, as the president has suggested and which is getting traction among Republicans right now?

COOKE: I don't know. I'm not quite sure whether we have thought this through. At what point do we think somebody is capable of exercising their own judgment? And I feel as if what's happened here is that we looked at the age of this guy in Florida—he was 19—and we said, well, we would like to stop that post hoc. And so why don't we change the age at which he would have been able to buy a rifle?

The fact that this guy was on the radar and there weren't any tools with which the local sheriff's office could stop him is a big problem. And that proposal, which has been picked up by Marco Rubio, among others, strikes me as the most fruitful one.

MARTIN: So this is the idea of expanding these so-called red flag laws that because so many people had warned about Nikolas Cruz's behavior, there were red flags, right? And a handful of states in this country have already passed these laws that say, listen, someone like Nikolas Cruz, a parent, a teacher, someone in his life, if they had alerted a judge, and a judge had made a decision that this young man should not have weapons, they could have removed those guns from him. Would you advocate a more expansive set of those laws across the country?

COOKE: Yes, absolutely, providing, of course, that there is sufficient due process. But I think, in this case, there would have been more than enough evidence. I mean, the big fear that gun owners have is that the system will be abused. So, for example, you know, I'm a semi-public figure. So someone will call the FBI and say, you know, Charles Cooke is crazy. He made this joke on Twitter, and he's probably going to shoot up a school.

But the point is that if that happened, a judge or a police officer would come and see me, and they would ask my wife and my employer and my friends and others whether I was a threat. And they would, of course, say no. But with Nikolas Cruz, they would have said yes.

MARTIN: You just explained a scenario in which you have faith in American institutions to some degree, and we are living in a moment where a lot of people don't. And, quite frankly, the NRA has spun up that fear, that paranoia that you will not get due process, that this will be left up to some subjective liberal judge who wants to strip you of your Second Amendment rights.

COOKE: Well, I think there are two reasons for that, and I think they're both fair. One is that often, when these laws are implemented, they are implemented by left-leaning politicians. The second thing here—and, again, I think Democrats have themselves to blame for this—is that you have seen over the last two years an almost endless push to restrict Second Amendment rights and strip them, in many cases, from people who the government has put on secret lists. Which is so flagrantly unconstitutional and is obviously going to inspire a lack of trust.

But again, that bill, when it was introduced, was defeated. Hopefully, it will be defeated again. And just because, you know, that bad idea has been put to the—doesn't mean that this can't be done correctly. I'd also just say, I do have a lot of faith in American institutions. Yes, maybe I have the optimist eye as an immigrant, but I think that our institutions are holding up pretty well.

MARTIN: What do you make of this moment writ large when you think about the gun debate in America and how it has been intractable for so many generations now? Do you think this is a moment where something might change if you agree that something should change?

COOKE: Well, as I say, I hope that the Cornyn-Murphy bill passes, which would fix the background check system. And I hope that we have some sort of gun violence restraining order bill. So I do hope something changes. I still think the gun debate is intractable, both because there are so many guns in circulation that it seems to me that we are always going to be tinkering around the edges and also because this issue has, over the years, largely been won by conservatives. And so to dismantle the victories that they have won would take such a long time, that even if you could somehow do it, I'm not convinced there would be a great change.

MARTIN: Charles, thanks so much for your time.

COOKE: Thank you for having me.

> *"Researcher compared yearly gun suicide and homicide rates over the 10 years following implementation of California's law with 32 control states that did not have such laws. They found 'no change in the rates of either cause of death from firearms through 2000.'"*

California Proves Background Checks Don't Work

Jon Miltimore

In the following viewpoint, Jon Miltimore argues that background checks do not lessen the number of gun deaths. The author uses statistics to cite what he perceives as strong gun control laws in California and the number of murders in that state as evidence. He also expresses what has become a typical complaint: that an American media that generally favors liberal gun control measures has ignored the findings in California. The author does concede that stricter background checks had the desired effects in two other states, however. Jon Miltimore is managing editor for the Foundation for Economic Education.

"California's Background Check Law Had No Impact on Gun Deaths, Johns Hopkins Study Finds," by Jon Miltimore, Foundation for Economic Education, December 5, 2018. https://fee.org/articles/california-s-background-check-law-had-no-impact-on-gun-deaths-johns-hopkins-study-finds/. Licensed under CC BY-ND 4.0 International.

As you read, consider the following questions:

1. Why did stricter background checks work in Missouri and Connecticut but not in California?
2. Why are more stringent background checks ineffective in limiting gun violence, according to the author?
3. Could there have been a flaw in the California law that contributed to a lack of success?

A new academic study has found that, once again, gun laws are not having their desired effect.

A joint study conducted by researchers at the Johns Hopkins Bloomberg School of Public Health and the University of California at Davis Violence Prevention Research Program found that California's much-touted mandated background checks had no impact on gun deaths, and researchers are puzzled as to why.

California Gun Laws Are a Failure

In 1991, California simultaneously imposed comprehensive background checks for firearm sales and prohibited gun sales (and gun possession) to people convicted of misdemeanor violent crimes. The legislation mandated that all gun sales, including private transactions, would have to go through a California-licensed Federal Firearms License (FFL) dealer. Shotguns and rifles, like handguns, became subject to a 15-day waiting period to make certain all gun purchasers had undergone a thorough background check.

It was the most expansive state gun control legislation in America, affecting an estimated one million gun buyers in the first year alone. Though costly and cumbersome, politicians and law enforcement agreed the law was worth it.

The legislation would "keep more guns out of the hands of the people who shouldn't have them," said then-Republican Gov. George Deukmejian.

"I think the new laws are going to help counter the violence," said LAPD spokesman William D. Booth.

More than a quarter of a century later, researchers at Johns Hopkins and UC Davis dug into the results of the sweeping legislation. Researchers compared yearly gun suicide and homicide rates over the 10 years following implementation of California's law with 32 control states that did not have such laws.

They found "no change in the rates of either cause of death from firearms through 2000."

The findings, which run counter to experiences in Missouri and Connecticut that did show a link between background checks and gun deaths, appear to have startled the researchers.

Garen Wintemute, a UC Davis professor of emergency medicine and senior author of the study, said incomplete data and flawed criminal record reporting might explain the results.

Wintemute noted:

In 1990, only 25 percent of criminal records were accessible in the primary federal database used for background checks, and centralized records of mental health prohibitions were almost nonexistent.

As a result, researchers said as many as one in four gun buyers may have purchased a firearm without undergoing a background check.

"We know at the individual level that comprehensive background check policies work, that they prevent future firearm violence at this level," said Nicole Kravitz-Wirtz, a researcher who led the survey.

Everyone Has Confirmation Bias, Even Experts

Perhaps unsurprisingly, the findings—which run counter to the conventional wisdom that gun control saves lives—have received almost no media attention.

An exception was the *Washington Post*, which cited the study (buried 20 paragraphs down) in an article in which the American

Medical Association calls for stronger gun control laws at the state level.

AMA President Barbara McAneny told the *Post* in an interview:

> We see this as an epidemic and public health crisis and we think intervening as early as possible is smarter than just building more intensive care units for people who are either killed or damaged and badly hurt by the violence.

Bizarrely, the *Post* cited the Johns Hopkins-UC Davis study as evidence that what "the AMA is calling for may be needed."

Apparently, to the *Washington Post*, California's failure to effectively enforce background checks that had no discernible impact on gun deaths is evidence that more gun control laws are needed.

Essentially, the study's authors, the AMA, and the *Post* appear incapable of seriously entertaining the possibility that sweeping gun control legislation might not have produced the results desired and expected: fewer deaths.

We Should Judge by Outcomes, Not Intentions

Alas, the experts are behaving exactly as expected.

More than a decade ago, the writer Louis Menand, in a *New Yorker* article, explained the rationalizations experts make when their theories fail to hold up in our real-world laboratory:

> When they're wrong, [experts are] rarely held accountable, and they rarely admit it, either. They insist that they were just off on timing, or blindsided by an improbable event, or almost right, or wrong for the right reasons. They have the same repertoire of self-justifications that everyone has, and are no more inclined than anyone else to revise their beliefs about the way the world works, or ought to work, just because they made a mistake.

California's failed gun control law appears to be yet another example of experts, to quote the great Milton Friedman, judging "policies and programs by their intentions rather than their results."

Despite the dismal record of gun control, expect the media and "experts" to use a repertoire of self-justifications rather than modify their beliefs—regardless of what the evidence shows.

> "Gun control is not a one-size-fits-all project; nor are there simple off the shelf solutions. Rather, policies have to be fitted to the problems and cultural contexts of particular societies. But first of all, societies have to acknowledge they have a problem."

International Gun Control Laws Show the Complexities of the Problem

Peter Squires

In the following viewpoint, Peter Squires argues the effectiveness of gun control on an international level. The author examines laws that target a wide range of weapons, including handguns and semiautomatic assault rifles. Among his focus topics is gang violence. He concludes that the issue is complex and that there is not one universal solution, but that every country must acknowledge their problems and arrive at laws and policies that work best for them. Peter Squires is professor of criminology and public policy at the University of Brighton.

As you read, consider the following questions:

1. What are "common sense" gun laws?
2. Does the author place any blame for the lack of gun control laws in the United States?
3. What evidence does the author give that gun control laws are working internationally?

This week brought news of yet another gun massacre in the United States at Washington Navy Yard. It is the latest in a string of 146 mass shootings, with more than 900 victims since 2006. The tragedy gives us pause to reflect on the "common sense" gun controls proposed by president Barack Obama but blocked by gun lobby senators only a few months ago.

Among other measures, Obama's proposals sought to reform the national firearm purchase check system, so that offenders and the mentally ill could not buy guns legally, and close down the unregulated secondary gun market which is such a handy supply line for the criminally inclined. No one is claiming such measures would have prevented Aaron Alexis from carrying out this particular rampage, but they are important features of any effective regime of public safety promotion that takes preventing gun violence seriously.

But does gun control actually work?

Evidence from the US itself shows a strong relationship between individual states with lax gun laws and higher than average rates of gun violence but despite apparent public support for sensible gun control, progress at the US Federal level currently seems unlikely. In this regard it is worth looking at what other countries, faced by gun violence, have made of gun control.

Guns and Values

A cautionary note is needed; gun control in many respects is a branch of crime prevention. A need for effective crime prevention is not invalidated by the argument that criminals break laws. If we had figured that one out, we criminologists could all go home.

The objective is to secure the most effective series of gun violence prevention measures; reducing risks consistent with our other social values. All things being equal, the more guns in a society, the greater the frequency of gun violence. But those "other values" and other social changes are important too. The more cohesive, trusting, tolerant and responsible a society is, the less risk that gun ownership itself represents.

Societies undergoing rapid social changes, or riven with conflicts and divisions are likely to become increasingly dangerous when firearms are added to the mix. Unfortunately these societies are often the very places where private citizens seek firearms for "self-defence" purposes.

To demonstrate the European range of gun homicide rates as compared with three other societies (Australia, Canada and India) and the USA: Norway, Sweden, Finland and Switzerland all have relatively high rates of gun ownership, likewise Canada and Australia, but nowhere near the US rates of gun violence. None of the European societies has been immune from the experience of "mass shooting" incidents and most have strengthened their guns laws as a consequence.

United Kingdom

Although a relatively low firearm ownership society, the UK has introduced significant changes over the past few decades, most notably banning semi-automatic rifles in 1988 and, subsequently, all handguns in 1998. Mass shootings at Hungerford and Dunblane respectively, rather than common gun crime prompted both reforms, but the changes occurred at a time of growing concern with street gang activity, rising criminal use of handguns and significant influxes of replica and realistic imitation air weapons.

For four years after 1998 these other trends overwhelmed the impact of the handgun ban but a series of other legislative changes and a steep learning curve by the police in proactive firearms control now reveal significant year on year reductions in gun crime in England and Wales. Handgun crime is now only half what it was a decade ago.

Canada

Canada also introduced tougher gun control measures, following the École Polytechnique Massacre in 1989. Tougher screening processes were introduced for all gun purchases including risk assessments, background checks and firearms registration. Later, further classes of firearms "not reasonably used in hunting" (prohibiting semi-automatic assault weapons) became restricted.

The new measures appeared to accelerate a downward trend in gun violence involving long weapons (rifles and shotguns) but also revealed a shift to handguns as criminal weapons of choice, as Canada also experienced an upsurge in street-gang problems. Tighter controls on handguns have also followed, having some positive impact over the past five years although, in this regard, Canada's efforts are rather undermined by the lax gun laws of its neighbour to the south. An overwhelming number of criminal handguns intercepted by the police in Canada are illegally sourced from the US.

Australia

Australia introduced much tighter gun controls in the wake of the Port Arthur massacre of 1996, although some Australian states had already begun to tighten their firearms controls following earlier episodes of gun violence.

Total gun homicide has tracked generally downwards since 1995, accelerating following the gun control and firearm buyback measures after 1996. Unfortunately a rise in criminal use of handguns (linked to serious and organised crime and criminal gang activity), fortunately dropping away after 2005-6, initially dwarfed the positive results of the 1996 reforms.

These brief case studies demonstrate conclusively that gun control can work, but it needs to be intelligently designed, effectively implemented and responsive to ongoing changes in criminal activity.

In each case, trafficking in handguns, developing gang cultures and changes at the level of global organised crime and criminal trafficking have threatened to undermine domestic successes. Gun control is not a one-size-fits-all project; nor are there simple off the shelf solutions. Rather, policies have to be fitted to the problems and cultural contexts of particular societies. But first of all, societies have to acknowledge they have a problem.

Periodical and Internet Sources Bibliography

The following articles have been selected to supplement the diverse views presented in this chapter.

BBC News, "America's Gun Culture in Charts," August 5, 2019. https://www.bbc.com/news/world-us-canada-41488081.

Matt Davis, "In Switzerland, Gun Ownership Is High but Mass Shootings Are Low. Why?" Big Think, March 17, 2019. https://bigthink.com/politics-current-affairs/switzerland-high-gun-ownership.

Gretchen Frazee, "What These Numbers Tell Us About the Gun Debate in 2019," PBS, September 3, 2019. https://www.pbs.org/newshour/nation/what-these-numbers-tell-us-about-the-gun-debate-in-2019.

German Lopez, "Study: Where Gun Laws Are Weaker, There Are More Mass Shootings," Vox, March 8, 2019. https://www.vox.com/2019/3/8/18254626/mass-shootings-gun-violence-laws-study.

John G. Malcolm and Amy Swearer, "6 Reasons Gun Control Will Not Solve Mass Killings," The National Interest, March 19, 2018. https://nationalinterest.org/blog/the-buzz/6-reasons-gun-control-will-not-solve-mass-killings-24975.

Megan Molteni, "The Looser a State's Gun Laws, the More Mass Shootings It Has," *Wired*, August 6, 2019. https://www.wired.com/story/the-looser-a-states-gun-laws-the-more-mass-shootings-it-has/.

Madeline Osburn, "Mass Shooting in Aurora Shows Why Gun Control Doesn't Work," The Federalist, February 20, 2019. https://thefederalist.com/2019/02/20/mass-shooting-aurora-shows-gun-control-doesnt-work/.

Anthony Zurcher, "US Guns Laws: Why It Won't Follow New Zealand's Lead," BBC News, March 21, 2019. https://www.bbc.com/news/world-us-canada-41489552.

OPPOSING
VIEWPOINTS®
SERIES

CHAPTER 3

How Important Is the Second Amendment?

Chapter Preface

No amendment to the United States Constitution has become more controversial than the Second Amendment, which has been left open to interpretation more than two hundred years after it was written.

The Second Amendment states:

A well regulated Militia, being necessary to the security of a free State, the right of the people to keep and bear Arms, shall not be infringed.

But times have changed quite a bit since those words were written. Would the founding fathers have framed the amendment identically had assault rifles rather than muskets been the weapons of choice during that period in history? And would they have added stipulations if a spate of mass shootings had murdered thousands of innocent citizens at that time?

Those that fear gun control measures in the United States often cite the Second Amendment as rock-solid proof that nothing should be done to limit access to guns of any kind. Those that disagree offer that the Second Amendment specifically states that the need for gun rights was based on the need to maintain a militia against those that practice tyranny. They point out that indeed times have changed.

Some believe the Second Amendment must provide protection for all those who wish to purchase guns. Others claim it should be interpreted to fit modern times. Still others feel it should be scrapped altogether as new and far more stringent anti-gun laws are enacted. The viewpoints expressed in the following chapter reflect the passionate opinions about these vague, few words written by men who would not recognize their country today.

"A growing body of research finds that the federal assault weapons ban— though only in effect for 10 years— had a positive impact on reducing both the use of assault weapons in crimes and the numbers of firearm injuries and fatalities in mass shootings."

Assault Weapons and High-Capacity Magazines Must Be Banned

Center for American Progress

In the following viewpoint, authors from the Center for American Progress argue that assault weapons with high-capacity magazines have no place in society and should be banned. The authors contend that such weapons are strictly weapons of war. Unlike hunting rifles and other guns, they have no use outside the battlefield and can only be used to kill people. The concern is that such weapons can not only be used for mass shootings but have grown increasingly menacing in inner-city gang violence as well. The Center for American Progress is a liberal public policy research and advocacy organization.

"Assault Weapons and High-Capacity Magazines Must Be Banned," Center for American Progress, August 12, 2019. Reprinted by permission.

As you read, consider the following questions:

1. Is this viewpoint convincing in its view that assault weapons have no use to civilian society?
2. How do the authors use statistics to argue for an assault weapons ban?
3. How could such a ban can be carried out, according to the viewpoint?

Assault weapons and high-capacity magazines have repeatedly been used to commit some of the worst mass shootings in modern US history, and they contribute to the daily toll of gun violence in communities around the country. They are weapons of war that have no place in civilian society. Congress must enact a federal ban on assault weapons and high-capacity magazines to keep these dangerous weapons out of US communities.

What Is an Assault Weapon?

Assault weapons are semi-automatic firearms—meaning that they fire a round every time the trigger is pulled—that are capable of accepting a detachable magazine and have another military-style feature such as a pistol grip, a folding stock, or a threaded barrel. Firearm manufacturers, in response to declining sales of handguns, began selling assault rifles in the civilian market in the 1980s as part of a broader effort to create a new market for military-style guns among civilian gun owners.[1]

What Is a High-Capacity Magazine?

A high-capacity magazine—also referred to as a large-capacity magazine—is a device that feeds ammunition into a firearm that holds more than 10 rounds of ammunition. A gun fitted with a high-capacity magazine can fire a higher number of bullets before needing to be reloaded. Today, models exist that can hold 20, 30, 50, or 100 rounds of ammunition in a single magazine. The functionality of high-capacity magazines has advanced in recent years, with the firearms and ammunition industry designing the devices to reduce the probability that ammunition will jam while multiple rounds are rapidly fired.[2] Magazines that accept more than 10 rounds of ammunition can be used in both long guns and handguns that accept detachable magazines.[3]

What Happens When an Assault Weapon with a High-Capacity Magazine Is Used in a Shooting?

The use of an assault weapon equipped with a high-capacity magazine increases the likelihood that a particular shooting will have a high death and injury count. These weapons are designed to fire bullets at higher velocities than handguns, increasing the lethality of shootings perpetrated with them.[4] An analysis of mass shootings committed from January 2009 through July 2015 found that when assault weapons or high-capacity magazines were used, 155 percent more people were shot, and 47 percent more people were killed.[5]

What Is the Current Federal Law Regarding Assault Weapons and High-Capacity Magazines?

There are currently no restrictions in federal law on the manufacture, sale, and possession of assault weapons and high-capacity magazines. In 1994, a federal ban was enacted on assault weapons and high-capacity magazines as part of the Violent Crime Control and Law Enforcement Act,[6] but it was allowed to expire in 2004.

Do Any States Ban Assault Weapons and High-Capacity Magazines?

Currently, seven states and Washington, D.C.[7] have laws banning assault weapons, while nine states and Washington, D.C. ban high-capacity magazines.[8] Yet these state-level efforts are undermined by the lack of a strong federal law banning these weapons. In July 2019, for example, a shooter shot 15 people, killing 3, in Gilroy, California, using an assault rifle purchased in Nevada. Although this firearm was banned and unavailable for sale in California, it was easily available in Nevada, which does not have a state-level assault weapons ban.[9]

Do Bans on Assault Weapons and High-Capacity Magazines Work?

A growing body of research finds that the federal assault weapons ban—though only in effect for 10 years—had a positive impact on reducing both the use of assault weapons in crimes and the numbers of firearm injuries and fatalities in mass shootings:

- In 2004, the US Department of Justice found that following the implementation of the ban, a number of cities and jurisdictions reported declines in the number of assault weapons recovered from crime scenes. These declines ranged from 17 percent to 72 percent.[10]
- Researchers analyzing public mass shootings from 1982 through 2011 found that both state and federal bans on assault weapons resulted in decreased rates of mass shooting fatalities. The federal ban also indicated a decrease in rates of mass shooting injuries.[11]
- A 2019 study examined mass shootings from 1981 through 2017 and analyzed the risk of fatalities in those incidents. The study found that during the 10-year period the federal ban was in effect, mass shooting fatalities were 70 percent less likely to occur than either before or after the ban.[12]
- Research from Stanford University reviewed US mass shootings[13] over a 35-year period. The analysis found that the decade during which the federal assault weapons ban was in effect was linked to a 25 percent decrease in mass shootings and a 40 percent decrease in mass shooting deaths.[14] Additionally, the research found that in the decade after the ban expired, mass shooting deaths increased by 347 percent.*[15]

The ban on high-capacity magazines within the federal assault weapons ban also had an impact:

- A *Washington Post* investigation of the impact of the federal ban in Virginia found that during the years it was in effect, there was a noted decline in the number of guns equipped with high-capacity magazines recovered from crime scenes; the rate reached a low of 10 percent in 2004. After the ban expired, this rate increased, reaching 20 percent in 2010.[16]
- A 2019 study analyzing mass shootings[17] that were committed between 1990 and 2017 found that 77 percent of mass shootings perpetrated with a high-capacity magazine occurred in states that did not have state-level bans on these specific ammunition-feeding devices.*[18]

What Happened When the Federal Ban Expired?

Following the expiration of the ban in 2004, assault weapons and high-capacity magazines once again became legal to manufacture and purchase, and the gun industry responded with renewed fervor, flooding the civilian consumer market with these guns. Since the expiration of the federal ban, assault weapons and high-capacity magazines have been used to perpetrate some of the deadliest public mass shootings in modern US history:

- On August 3, 2019, in El Paso, Texas, 46 people were shot, 22 fatally.[19]
- On February 14, 2018, in Parkland, Florida, 34 people were shot, 17 fatally.[20]
- On November 5, 2017, in Sutherland Springs, Texas, 46 people were shot, 26 fatally.[21]
- On October 1, 2017, in Las Vegas, 480 people were shot, 58 fatally.[22]
- On June 12, 2016, in Orlando, Florida, 102 people were shot, 49 fatally.[23]
- On December 14, 2012, in Newtown, Connecticut, 28 people were shot, 26 fatally.[24]

- On July 20, 2012, in Aurora, Colorado, 70 people were shot, 12 fatally.[25]

Not only do these highly dangerous firearms and accessories continue to be used in horrific mass-casualty shootings, they are increasingly being used in cities that experience high rates of gun violence. A 2017 study found that guns equipped with high-capacity magazines made up between 22 percent and 36 percent of crime guns in the United States.[26] A 2010 report from the Police Executive Research Forum noted that more than one-third of US police agencies reported increased use of assault weapons following the expiration of the federal ban.[27] In 2018, Baltimore Interim Police Commissioner Gary Tuggle stated that one-third of guns recovered in criminal investigations were equipped with high-capacity magazines. The Baltimore Police Department recovered 890 firearms with high-capacity magazines from January 1, 2017, through April 29, 2018.[28]

The ban's expiration has also been linked to changes in international firearms trafficking. Assault weapons and high-capacity magazines are desirable weapons for organized crime and cartels in Mexico.[29] A 2013 study found that following the expiration of the ban, Mexican municipalities bordering Texas, Arizona, and New Mexico reported increased levels of gun homicides. Municipalities near California did not see similar increases, likely due in part to the state-level ban on assault weapons.[30]

* Update, November 5, 2019: This fact sheet has been updated to reflect research published in fall 2019 on the efficacy of the federal assault weapons ban and of state-level bans of high-capacity magazines in the United States.

Endnotes

1. Violence Policy Center, "The Militarization of the US Civilian Firearms Market" (Washington: 2011), available at http://vpc.org/studies/militarization.pdf.

2. Alain Stephens, "The Gun Industry Is Betting on Bigger High-Capacity Magazines," The Trace, June 12, 2019, available at

https://www.thetrace.org/2019/06/gun-industry-high-capacity-magazine-size/.

3. Giffords Law Center, "Large Capacity Magazines," available at https://lawcenter.giffords.org/gun-laws/policy-areas/hardware-ammunition/large-capacity-magazines/ (last accessed August 2019).

4. Elizerie de Jager, Eric Goralnick, and Justin C. McCarty, "Lethality of Civilian Active Shooter Incidents With and Without Semiautomatic Rifles in the United States," *Journal of the American Medical Association* 320 (10) (2018): 1034–1035, available at https://jamanetwork.com/journals/jama/fullarticle/2702134.

5. Everytown for Gun Safety, "Analysis of Recent Mass Shootings" (New York: 2015), available at https://everytownresearch.org/documents/2015/04/analysis-of-recent-mass-shootings.pdf.

6. Public Safety and Recreational Firearms Use Protection Act, within the Violent Crime Control and Law Enforcement Act of 1994, H.R. 3355, 103rd Cong., 1st sess. (October 26, 1993), available at https://www.congress.gov/bill/103rd-congress/house-bill/3355.

7. California, Connecticut, Hawaii, Maryland, Massachusetts, New Jersey, and New York are the only states with legislation banning some form of assault weapons. Giffords Law Center, "Assault Weapons: Summary of State Law," available at https://lawcenter.giffords.org/gun-laws/policy-areas/hardware-ammunition/assault-weapons/#state (last accessed August 2019).

8. California, Colorado, Connecticut, Hawaii, Maryland, Massachusetts, New Jersey, New York, and Vermont are the only states with legislation banning high-capacity magazines. Giffords Law Center, "Large Capacity Magazines: Summary of State Law," available at https://lawcenter.giffords.org/gun-laws/policy-areas/hardware-ammunition/large-capacity-magazines/#state (last accessed August 2019).

9. Dan Simon, Eric Levenson, and Darran Simon, "Assault-style rifle used in Gilroy shooting could not be sold in California, state attorney general says," CNN, July 29, 2019, available at https://www.cnn.com/2019/07/29/us/gilroy-california-food-festival-shooting-monday/index.html.

10. The study examined Baltimore; Miami; Milwaukee; Boston; St. Louis; and Anchorage, Alaska. Christopher S. Koper, "Updated

Assessment on the Federal Assault Weapons Ban: Impacts on Gun Markets and Gun Violence, 1994-2003" (Washington: US Department of Justice, 2004), available at https://www.ncjrs.gov/pdffiles1/nij/grants/204431.pdf.

11. Mark Gius, "The Impact of State and Federal Assault Weapons Bans on Public Mass Shootings," Applied Economics Letters 22 (4) (2014): 281–284, available at http://www.tandfonline.com/doi/abs/10.1080/13504851.2014.939367.

12. Charles DiMaggio and others, "Changes in US mass shooting deaths associated with the 1994-2004 federal assault weapons ban," *Journal of Trauma and Acute Care Surgery* 86 (1) (2019): 11–19, available at https://www.ncbi.nlm.nih.gov/pubmed/30188421.

13. The researchers defined a mass shooting as an incident in which a shooter killed six or more people in a public setting.

14. John Donohue and Theodora Boulouta, "That Assault Weapon Ban? It Really Did Work," *The New York Times*, September 4, 2019, available at https://www.nytimes.com/2019/09/04/opinion/assault-weapon-ban.html.

15. Ibid.

16. David Fallis, "Data indicate drop in high-capacity magazines during federal gun ban," *The Washington Post*, January 10, 2013, available at https://www.washingtonpost.com/investigations/data-point-to-drop-in-high-capacity-magazines-during-federal-gun-ban/2013/01/10/d56d3bb6-4b91-11e2-a6a6-aabac85e8036_story.html.

13. The researchers defined a mass shooting as an incident in which a shooter killed six or more people.

18. Louis Klarevas, Andrew Conner, and David Hemenway, "The Effect of Large-Capacity Magazine Bans on High-Fatality Mass Shootings, 1990–2017," *American Journal of Public Health* (2019): e1–e8, available at https://ajph.aphapublications.org/doi/10.2105/AJPH.2019.305311.

19. Chas Danner, "Everything we know about the El Paso Walmart massacre," *New York Magazine* Intelligencer, August 5, 2019, available at http://nymag.com/intelligencer/2019/08/everything-we-know-about-the-el-paso-walmart-shooting.html.

20. Evan Perez, "Florida school shooter could have fired many more bullets," CNN, February 27, 2018, available at https://www.cnn.com/2018/02/27/us/florida-school-shooter-ammunition-left/index.html.

21. Matt Pearce and John Savage, "26 dead in Texas church shooting, with children among the victims," *Los Angeles Times*, November 5, 2017, available at https://www.latimes.com/nation/nationnow/la-na-texas-church-shooting-20171105-htmlstory.html.

22. *The New York Times*, "Multiple weapons found in Las Vegas gunman's hotel room," October 2, 2017, available at https://www.nytimes.com/2017/10/02/us/las-vegas-shooting.html.

23. Bart Jansen, "Weapons gunman used in Orlando shooting are high-capacity, common," *USA Today*, June 14, 2016, available at https://www.usatoday.com/story/news/2016/06/14/guns-used-kill-49-orlando-high-capacity-common-weapons/85887260.

24. Steve Almasy, "Newtown shooter's guns: what we know," CNN, December 19, 2012, available at https://www.cnn.com/2012/12/18/us/connecticut-lanza-guns/index.html.

25. Dan Frosch and Kirk Johnson, "Gunman kills 12 in Colorado, reviving gun debate," *The New York Times*, July 20, 2012, available at https://www.nytimes.com/2012/07/21/us/shooting-at-colorado-theater-showing-batman-movie.html.

26. Christopher Koper and others, "Criminal Use of Assault Weapons and High-Capacity Semiautomatic Firearms: an Updated Examination of Local and National Sources," *Journal of Urban Health* 95 (3) (2018): 313–321, available at https://link.springer.com/article/10.1007/s11524-017-0205-7.

27. Police Executive Research Forum, "Guns and Crime: Breaking New Ground by Focusing on the Local Impact" (Washington: 2010), available at http://www.policeforum.org/assets/docs/Critical_Issues_Series/guns%20and%20crime%20-%20breaking%20new%20ground%20by%20focusing%20on%20the%20local%20impact%202010.pdf.

28. Police Executive Research Forum, "Reducing Gun Violence: What Works, and What Can Be Done Now" (Washington: 2019), available at https://www.policeforum.org/assets/reducinggunviolence.pdf.

29. Colby Goodman and Michel Marizco, "US Firearms Trafficking to Mexico: New Data and Insights Illuminate Key Trends and Challenges," in Eric L. Olson, David A. Shirk, and Andrew Selee, eds., *Shared Responsibility: US-Mexico Policy Options for Confronting Organized Crime* (Washington: Woodrow Wilson International Institute for Scholars Mexico Institute and San Diego: University of San Diego Trans-Border Institute, 2010), available at http://www.wilsoncenter.org/sites/default/files/Shared%20Responsibility%2012.22.10.pdf.

30. Arindrajit Dube, Oeindrila Dube, and Omar García-Ponce, "Cross-Border Spillover: US Gun Laws and Violence in Mexico," *American Political Science Review* 107 (3) (2013): 397–417, available at http://odube.net/papers/Cross_border_spillover.pdf.

> *"Going to a gun range and shooting
> a few times does not make you
> well equipped to deal with violent
> situations where your adrenaline is
> going like crazy, your heart is beating
> a mile a minute, and you have
> seconds to make the right decision.
> It takes good training—repetition,
> practicing over and over—to react to
> that kind of situation."*

"More People with Guns" Won't Help

Colleen Walsh

In the following viewpoint, Colleen Walsh interviews Harvard University public health professor David Hemenway to get his thoughts about the most effective methods of combating the rise of mass shootings in the United States. Hemenway cites the success of foreign countries that have instituted gun control laws and claims the "good guy with the gun" philosophy to be folly. He laments that everyday people, most of whom favor stronger gun laws that include universal background checks, cannot find a way to make a bigger impact on public policy. Colleen Walsh is a staff writer for The Harvard Gazette.

As you read, consider the following questions:

1. Does David Hemenway believe the fear that gun control advocates want to take away the guns of responsible people is warranted?
2. How does Hemenway think gun violence in the media has affected the debate over gun control?
3. What does Hemingway think about a multidimensional approach to stopping gun violence?

The mass shootings over the weekend in El Paso, Texas, and Dayton, Ohio, killed at least 31 people and wounded scores more. Those incidents were just the latest such deadly attacks in the United States, which has tallied more than 250 since Jan. 1, according to a new report by Gun Violence Archive. The group defines a mass shooting as one that claims the lives of at least four victims. David Hemenway, professor of health policy at Harvard T.H. Chan School of Public Health, director of the Harvard Injury Control Research Center, and author of the 2006 book "Private Guns, Public Health," has spent much of his career studying gun violence. He spoke with the *Gazette* recently about what can be done to stop mass shootings.

GAZETTE: How do other countries, where mass killings are less common, handle gun issues differently?

HEMENWAY: First, it's important to recognize the other high-income countries start off with many fewer guns and much stronger gun laws. Second, often when there is a mass shooting in another country it's a time when everyone is thinking about guns, and it becomes an opportunity to think about what kinds of gun laws are needed. Typically it is a time when countries improve their gun laws, making them stronger, not solely to prevent mass shootings but to also to help prevent other firearm-related problems, such as homicides, suicides, gun robbery, gun intimidations, and gun accidents.

GAZETTE: How do you respond to the suggestion that shooters would be dispatched more quickly and inflict fewer injuries if more people carried weapons?

HEMENWAY: Too many of us watch television shows and movies where guns are the solution to so many problems. The good guy with the gun is the big hero. One huge problem is that so many people in the US are armed who really aren't well trained. Going to a gun range and shooting a few times does not make you well equipped to deal with violent situations where your adrenaline is going like crazy, your heart is beating a mile a minute, and you have seconds to make the right decision. It takes good training—repetition, practicing over and over—to react to that kind of situation. You can't, on the fly, suddenly think you are going to be this great hero; instead you could shoot the wrong person, or you could get in the way of the police or others who are well trained and trying to figure out what's going on. Most people, unless they are with the armed services or a member of the police force, never encounter such violent scenarios. So it's going to be incredibly rare for you to be in a situation where you could actually do something. Do we really want continuously to train millions of people for an event that virtually almost none of them will ever encounter? Even for something as simple as CPR, continued training is needed. I was taught CPR 10 years ago, but I don't feel at all confident that I would really know what to do if I was alone and had only seconds to respond effectively. For mass shootings you would have to keep training over and over for the training to be at all effective.

GAZETTE: Some gun control opponents have pointed to mental health issues and violent video games as major factors in the number of mass shootings in the United States. Are those two things more prevalent here than in other countries with lower rates of gun violence, and, if so, why?

HEMENWAY: There are a whole range of things that could play a role in prevention, including better parenting, less racism, better education, more job opportunities. All of these things might have some effect on reducing shootings in the US. We should improve all those things. But the most cost-effective interventions involve doing something about guns. For example, as far as we can tell, virtually all developed countries have violent video games and people with mental health issues. There's no evidence that I know of that shows that people in the US have more mental health issues, especially violent mental health issues. Compared to other high-income countries we are just average in terms of non-gun crime and non-gun violence. The elephant in the room, the thing that makes us stand out among the 29 other high-income countries, is our guns and our weak gun laws. As a result, we have many more gun-related problems than any other high-income country. Every other developed country has shown us the way to vastly reduce our problems. Our guns, and our permissive gun laws, are what make us different than France, Italy, the Netherlands, South Korea, New Zealand, you name it.

GAZETTE: Why does it seem many law-abiding American gun owners fear restrictions like background checks and the elimination of high-capacity magazines, bump stocks, and assault rifles? How would most gun owners be affected by such changes?

HEMENWAY: The overwhelming majority of American gun owners favor universal background checks, at least that is what they say on survey after survey. Most favor the elimination of military weapons in everybody's hands. If you asked them whether they feel comfortable with some of the people in this country who own guns legally, they would say "no." Just as there are some bad drivers, there are also some irresponsible gun owners. A problem

> *"Some say the framers only meant
> to protect well-organized militias in
> the respective states, forerunners of
> today's National Guard. Others say
> the framers also intended to shield
> the guns of individuals, the weapons
> they would use if those militias were
> called upon to fight."*

Repealing the Second Amendment Is Not a Simple Prospect

Ron Elving

In the following viewpoint, Ron Elving explains what has been perceived as an overwhelming process to overturn the Second Amendment. The author offers a warning to those who believe the Second Amendment should be abolished that it would take a level of consensus from states and national government officials that seems unlikely to be achieved in nearly any political landscape, but especially in the divisive times of the Trump administration. Ron Elving is senior editor and correspondent for National Public Radio (NPR).

"Repeal the Second Amendment? That's Not So Simple. Here's What It Would Take," by Ron Elving, National Public Radio Inc. (NPR), March 1, 2018. Reprinted by permission.

As you read, consider the following questions:

1. Is abolishing the Second Amendment realistic, according to the viewpoint?
2. What changes would have to be made in the mindset of US government officials for the Second Amendment to be banned?
3. Does the author indicate his interpretation of the Second Amendment?

T he Second Amendment."
    If you've lived in America, you've heard those words spoken with feeling.

The feeling may have been forceful, even vehement.

"Why? The Second Amendment, that's why."

The same words can be heard uttered in bitterness, as if in blame.

"Why? The Second Amendment, that's why."

Or then again, with reverence, an invocation of the sacred—rather like "the Second Coming."

Talk of gun rights and gun control is back on full boil after 17 people were killed in the Parkland, Fla., school shooting, so the conversation turns to the Second Amendment quickly and often.

We are talking, of course, about the Second Amendment to US Constitution, in the Bill of Rights.

It reads in full:

A well-regulated militia, being necessary to the security of a free State, the right of the people to keep and bear Arms, shall not be infringed.

Simple. And not simple. Assuming it means just what it says, just what does it actually say?

Scholars have parsed the words, and courts and lawyers have argued over their meaning. Historians have debated what was meant by "well-regulated militia" back in 1789.

Some say the framers only meant to protect well-organized militias in the respective states, forerunners of today's National Guard. Others say the framers also intended to shield the guns of individuals, the weapons they would use if those militias were called upon to fight.

Heller Brings Some Clarity

To some extent, the issue was clarified, if not settled, by the *Heller* decision of the US Supreme Court in 2008. The 5-4 decision held that the Second Amendment meant individuals had an inherent right to own guns for lawful purposes.

Heller applied that standard to overturn a ban on privately held handguns, enacted in the District of Columbia. But the same basic reasoning has also been used to defend the private ownership of AR-15-type rifles such as the one used in Parkland and other mass shootings in recent years.

Congress tried to ban "assault-style" weapons in 1994 but put a 10-year sunset provision in the law. It survived court challenges at the time, but when the 10-year term had passed, the majority control of Congress had also passed—from the Democrats, who had enacted the ban, to the Republicans, who let it lapse.

Since then, all efforts to restrict the sale of such weapons have failed. Even relatively bipartisan attempts at strengthening other restrictions, such as the Manchin-Toomey background check expansion bill in 2013, have fallen short of the necessary supermajority needed for passage in the Senate.

It was not, as President Trump alleged Wednesday, because of a lack of "presidential backup." President Barack Obama supported the bill, as Sen. Pat Toomey, a Pennsylvania Republican, pointed out to Trump. Republicans filibustered the bill, which got 54 votes.

In each case, defenders of gun rights have invoked the Second Amendment, the text that casts a long shadow across all discussions of guns in the US. At times, it seems to all but end such discussion.

Parkland Changes Calculus

But now, the tide is running the other way. The Parkland shootings have created a new moment and a new movement, led by teenagers who survived the tragedy and took their protests to social media and beyond.

Suddenly, even Trump is tossing out ideas about keeping students safe, arming teachers, restraining gun sales through background checks and higher age limits, and even banning accessories such as "bump stocks" that enable nonautomatic weapons to fire rapidly and repeatedly.

And it's still unclear what Trump wants exactly. Republicans on Capitol Hill seem flummoxed by Trump's posture.

After Trump's made-for-cable bipartisan meeting at the White House with members of Congress, Texas Republican John Cornyn, a leader on gun issues in the Senate, seemed to scratch his head.

"I think everybody is trying to absorb what we just heard," Cornyn told reporters. "He's a unique president, and I think if he was focused on a specific piece of legislation rather than a grab bag of ideas, then I think he could have a lot of influence, but right now we don't have that."

He added that he didn't think simply because the president says he supports something that it would pass muster with Republicans. "I wouldn't confuse what he said with what can actually pass," Cornyn said. "I don't expect to see any great divergence in terms of people's views on the Second Amendment, for example."

Ah, and there are those two words again—Second Amendment.

If new restrictions are enacted—a prospect far from certain, as Cornyn rightly points out—they will surely be tested in the courts. There, it will be argued that they infringe on the rights of law-abiding citizens to "keep and bear" firearms.

In other words, they will run afoul of, that's right, the Second Amendment.

Anticipating that, some gun control advocates—and at least one lifelong Republican—want to leap to the ultimate battlement and do it now. They want to repeal, or substantially alter, the formidable amendment itself.

That would seem logical, at least to these advocates. If some 70 percent of Americans want more gun control and the Second Amendment stands in their way, why shouldn't they be able to do something about it?

Someday, it is conceivable, the people and politicians of the United States may be ready for that. But it will need to be a very different United States than we know today.

Why? Because amendments to the Constitution, once ratified, become fully part of the Constitution. Changing or removing them requires a two-stage process that has proved historically difficult.

The Founding Fathers were willing to be edited, it seems, but they did not want it to be easy. So they made the amending process a steep uphill climb, requiring a clear national consensus to succeed.

Why It Takes Consensus

A proposed amendment to the Constitution must first be passed by Congress with two-thirds majorities in *both* the House and the Senate.

The two chambers have not achieved such a margin for a newly written amendment to the Constitution in nearly half a century. The last such effort was the 26th Amendment (lowering the voting age nationwide from 21 to 18), and it cleared Capitol Hill in March 1971.

(There has been another amendment added since, in 1992, but it had been written and approved by Congress literally generations ago. More about that curious "zombie" amendment below.)

Even after surviving both chambers of Congress in 1971, the 18-year-old vote amendment still had to survive the second stage of the process—the more difficult stage.

Just like all the other amendments before it, the new voting age had to be ratified by three-fourths of the states. That is currently at least 38 states. Another way to look at it: If as few as 13 states refuse, the amendment stalls.

This arduous process has winnowed out all but a handful of the amendments proposed over the past 230 years. Every Congress produces scores of proposals, sometimes well over 100. The 101st Congress (1989 to 1991) produced 214.

Some deal with obscure concerns; many address facets of the electoral process—especially the Electoral College and the choosing of a president. Many are retreads from earlier sessions of Congress. The one thing most have in common is that they never even come to a vote.

Two That Fell Short

In 1995, a watershed year with big new GOP majorities in both chambers, two major constitutional amendments were brought to votes in the Capitol. One would have imposed term limits on members of Congress. It failed to get even close to two-thirds in the House, so the Senate did not bother.

The other proposed amendment would have required the federal government to balance its budget, not in theory down the road but in reality and in real time. It quickly got two-thirds in the House but failed to reach that threshold in the Senate by a single vote (one Republican in the chamber voted no).

So even relatively popular ideas with a big head of steam can hit the wall of the amendment process. How much more challenging would it be to tackle individual gun ownership in a country where so many citizens own guns—and care passionately about their right to do so?

Overcoming the NRA and other elements of the gun lobby is only the beginning. The real obstacle would be tremendous support for guns in Southern, Western and rural Midwestern states, which would easily total up to more than enough states to block a gun control amendment.

There have been six amendments that got the needed margins in House and Senate but not the needed margin of support in the state legislatures. The most recent was the Equal Rights Amendment,

THE SECOND AMENDMENT WAS WRITTEN BEFORE WE HAD A MILITARY

Much of the discussion following the Newtown tragedy has centered on the second part of the Second Amendment: "the right to keep and bear arms shall not be infringed."

There has been little mention of the initial phrase: "A well regulated Militia being necessary to the security of a free State."

At the time the amendment was drafted, security depended on every head of household being able to grab a musket and run out into the street to fight off invaders.

Today, our national security depends upon a variety of sophisticated weapons and thousands of troops trained in how to use them.

Since the Constitution does not mention hunting or self-defense, state and federal legislation must draw a clear distinction between weapons needed for those purposes and weapons appropriate only for military use.

Possession of military weapons should be restricted to the armed forces, and the circumstances under which private ownership of guns are permitted for hunting or self-defense should be clarified.

It should be possible to accomplish this without accusing each other of violating the Constitution.

"LETTER: 2nd Amendment Written Before We Had a Military to Protect Us," by Nancy Beals, Hamden, Hearst, January 31, 2013.

---

a remarkably simple statement ("Equality of rights under the law shall not be denied or abridged by the United States or any State on account of sex") that cleared Congress with bipartisan support in 1972 and quickly won nods from most of the states.

But in the mid-1970s, a resistance campaign began and stymied the ERA in many of the remaining states. The resistance then managed to persuade several states to rescind their ratification votes. With momentum now reversed, the ERA died when its window for ratification closed.

Zombie Amendments

Other amendments that met similar fates included one granting statehood to the District of Columbia. Like the ERA, the D.C. amendment had a time limit for ratification that expired. But other amendments sent out for ratification in the past did not have a limit, and so might still be ratified—at least theoretically.

The granddaddy of these "zombie" amendments was the very first among the Bill of Rights, which began with 12 items rather than 10. The proposed amendment sought to regulate the number of constituents to be represented by a member of the House, and its numbers were soon outdated. So it has never been ratified and presumably will not be.

The one other amendment originally proposed in 1789 but not ratified as part of the original 10 amendments sat around for generations. Then it caught the attention of state legislatures in the late 1980s, at a time of popular reaction against pay raises for Congress. This amendment stated that a member of Congress who voted for a pay raise could not receive that raise until after the next election for the House of Representatives.

That amendment was dusted off and recirculated, and it reached the ratification threshold in 1992, more than 200 years after it had first been proposed. It is now the 27th Amendment to the Constitution, and the last—at least so far.

A New Constitutional Convention?

If all this seems daunting, as it should, there is one alternative for changing the Constitution. That is the calling of a Constitutional Convention. This, too, is found in Article V of the Constitution and allows for a new convention to bypass Congress and address issues of amendment on its own.

To exist with this authority, the new convention would need to be called for by two-thirds of the state legislatures.

So if 34 states saw fit, they could convene their delegations and start writing amendments. Some believe such a convention would have the power to rewrite the entire 1787 Constitution, if it saw fit. Others say it would and should be limited to specific issues or targets, such as term limits or balancing the budget—or changing the campaign-finance system or restricting the individual rights of gun owners.

There have been calls for an "Article V convention" from prominent figures on the left as well as the right. But there are those on both sides of the partisan divide who regard the entire proposition as suspect, if not frightening.

One way or another, any changes made by such a powerful convention would need to be ratified by three-fourths of the states—just like amendments that might come from Congress.

And three-fourths would presumably be as high a hurdle for convention-spawned amendments as it has been for those from Congress—dating to the 1700s.

> "For most of the republic's lifespan,
> from 1791 to 2008, those commas
> and clauses were debated by
> attorneys and senators, slave
> owners and freedmen, judges,
> Black Panthers, governors and
> lobbyists. For some, the militia was
> key; for others the right that shall
> not be infringed; for yet others,
> the question of states versus the
> federal government."

The Second Amendment Is Open to Interpretation

Alan Yuhas

In the following viewpoint Alan Yuhas explores what the founding fathers meant when they wrote the Second Amendment to the Constitution and how Supreme Court interpretations have altered how Congress and the American people have argued the subject of gun control. The author delves into the debate between those that claim that the right to bear arms shall not be infringed should still be taken literally today and those who feel that the framers who targeted the need for a well-regulated militia make the document no longer relevant. Alan Yuhas is a former reporter for the Guardian. *He currently is senior staff editor for the* New York Times.

"The Right to Bear Arms: What Does the Second Amendment Really Mean?" by Alan Yuhas, Guardian News and Media Limited, October 5, 2017. Reprinted by permission.

As you read, consider the following questions:

1. Does the author maintain objectivity throughout this piece?
2. How have the courts and Congress changed how Americans have interpreted the Second Amendment over the years?
3. How have issues facing the United States in various eras altered laws regarding the Second Amendment?

The second amendment has become a badge and bumper sticker, a shield for gun activists and scripture for much of the American right. But like other cherished texts, it is not as clear as many make it out to be.

The amendment reads: "A well regulated militia, being necessary to the security of a free state, the right of the people to keep and bear arms, shall not be infringed."

For most of the republic's lifespan, from 1791 to 2008, those commas and clauses were debated by attorneys and senators, slave owners and freedmen, judges, Black Panthers, governors and lobbyists. For some, the militia was key; for others the right that shall not be infringed; for yet others, the question of states versus the federal government. For the most part, the supreme court stayed out it.

"Americans have been thinking about the second amendment as an individual right for generations," said Adam Winkler, a law professor at UCLA and author of *Gunfight: The Battle over the Right to Bear Arms in America*. "You can find state supreme courts in the mid-1800s where judges say the second amendment protects an individual right."

But for the 70 years or so before a supreme court decision in 2008, he said, "the supreme court and federal courts held that it only applied in the context of militias, the right of states to protect themselves from federal interference."

In 2008, the supreme court decided the *District of Columbia v Heller*, 5-4, overturning a handgun ban in the city. The conservative justice Antonin Scalia wrote the opinion in narrow but unprecedented terms: for the first time in the country's history, the supreme court explicitly affirmed an individual's right to keep a weapon at home for self-defense.

Justice John Paul Stevens dissented, saying the decision showed disrespect "for the well-settled views of all of our predecessors on the court, and for the rule of law itself." Two years later, he dissented from another decision favoring gun rights, writing:

> The reasons that motivated the framers to protect the ability of militiamen to keep muskets, or that motivated the Reconstruction Congress to extend full citizenship to freedmen in the wake of the Civil War, have only a limited bearing on the question that confronts the homeowner in a crime-infested metropolis today.

This fight over history, waged by supreme court justices and unlikely allies and foes, goes all the way back.

"People look at the same record and come to wildly different conclusions about what the view was in the 18th century, in the 19th century," said Nicholas Johnson, a Fordham University law professor who argues against Winkler's view of 20th-century case law.

Attempts to parse "original" intent go all the way back to the revolution and its aftermath, when the country's founders bickered about what exactly they were talking about. Carl Bogus, a law professor at Roger Williams University, has argued that James Madison wrote the second amendment in part to reassure his home state of Virginia, where slave owners were terrified of revolts and wary of northerners who would undermine the system.

"The militia were at that stage almost exclusively a slave-control tool in the south," he said. "You gave Congress the power to arm the militia—if Congress chooses not to arm our militia, well, we all know what happens."

The federalist Madison's compromise, according to Bogus, was to promise a bill of rights. After weeks of tense debate, his federalists narrowly won the vote to ratify the constitution. "He writes an amendment that gives the states the right to have an armed militia, by the people arming themselves."

A year later, the federal government passed a law requiring every man eligible for his local militia to acquire a gun and register with authorities. (The law was only changed in 1903.)

After the civil war, second amendment rights were again debated by Congress, which abolished militias in the former Confederate states and passed the 1866 Civil Rights Act, explicitly protecting freed slaves' right to bear arms. A century later, the founders of the Black Panthers took up guns, symbolically and literally, to press for equal civil rights in California.

The state's conservative lawmakers promptly took up the cause of gun control. In 1967, Governor Ronald Reagan signed the Mulford Act, banning the public carry of loaded guns in cities. The governor said he saw "no reason why on the street today a citizen should be carrying loaded weapons."

Reagan later supported the Brady Act, a gun control law named after his aide, who was shot during an assassination attempt on Reagan in Washington DC. The National Rifle Association supported the Mulford Act but opposed the Brady Act, signed into law 26 years later.

Winkler, the UCLA professor, said that during the 1970s, a "revolt among the membership profoundly altered the NRA overnight. Since the 1930s, the group had supported restrictions on machine guns and public carry, but angry hardliners took control over the organization in 1977, when moderates wanted to retreat from lobbying work. The group then began a decades-long campaign to popularize its uncompromising positions.

"The NRA goes far beyond what the second amendment requires—people walking around with permits, on college campuses," Winkler said. "Their argument is it's a fundamental right and freedom. People care more about values than they care about policy."

In the late 1990s, several prominent liberal attorneys, such as Laurence Tribe and Akhil Reed Amar, also argued for an individual right while advocating gun regulation. Gun control activists say they have not changed tack since the supreme court's 2008 decision. Scalia wrote a narrow opinion and listed several exceptions, such as bans on "unusual and dangerous weapons" and sales to domestic abusers and people with mental illness. He also wrote that states and cities could ban firearms from places like government buildings.

Lower courts have upheld many gun laws around the country since 2008, and the supreme court has declined to hear any second amendment cases since 2010. Attorneys and activists on both sides expect a looming fight over the right to carry guns in public, which the *Heller* decision does not address.

"The courts generally strike a balance between the need for lawmakers to protect public safety and this notion of second amendment rights," said Avery Gardiner, co-president of the Brady Campaign to Prevent Gun Violence. The *Heller* decision, she said, was "entirely consistent" with gun laws like background checks.

"There's a mythology here that the supreme court has said something about the second amendment that it hasn't," she said. "I think most Americans don't like reading the footnotes."

> "We need not and indeed should not fall victim to one more of the European ailments: the disarming of the people under the dangerous notion that the private citizenry cannot be trusted and should not be allowed to have the means of self-defense."

The Rights Guaranteed by the Second Amendment Must Be Defended

Richard Ebeling

In the following viewpoint, Richard Ebeling argues for a literal interpretation of the Second Amendment. Citing historical examples such as confiscation of guns in the Communist Soviet Union and the Warsaw Rebellion, in which Jewish ghetto fighters bravely used weapons to battle back against the Nazis, the author maintains that the right to bear arms prevents one-sided victimization and tyranny. His argument is not an eye for an eye, but rather the notion that everyone should be allowed to defend themselves from attackers. Richard Ebeling is professor of economics at Northwood University in Michigan.

"The Importance of the Second Amendment," by Richard Ebeling, May 30, 2014. Reprinted by permission.

As you read, consider the following questions:

1. Are there flaws in the theory that people must be allowed to carry guns to defend themselves?
2. Would more guns in the hands of private citizens have altered tragic outcomes, according to the author?
3. How does the author interpret the Second Amendment in modern society?

For millions of Americans the Second Amendment and its guarantee of the right of the individual to bear arms appears irrelevant and practically anachronistic. It seems a throwback to those earlier days of the Wild West, when many men, far from the law and order provided by the town sheriff and circuit judge, had to protect their families and land from cattle rustlers and outlaw bands. Such people are wrong.

If in our contemporary world the law fails to do its job of seeing that the guilty pay for their crimes, we take solace in the fantasy of extralegal solutions. We imagine that somewhere there is a Clint Eastwood on a metropolitan police force who uses some "magnum force" to see to it that the perpetrator of a crime doesn't go unpunished. Or we want to think that there is a Charles Bronson occasionally roaming the streets of a large city at night fulfilling the "death wish" of the street criminal whom local law enforcement is not able to punish.

The crime once having been committed, it is some breakdown in the judicial system that prevents justice from being served. If only the law didn't coddle the criminal or allow his defense attorney to use "loopholes" in the law, no criminal would ever escape his just deserts.

This popular conception of the legal system, law enforcement, and government, however, suffers from two fundamental flaws: first, it focuses on the legal process (and any supposed weaknesses in it) only after a crime has been committed; and second, it ignores completely the fact that it might be the government itself that is the potential perpetrator of crimes against the American citizenry.

The Tragedy of the Unarmed Victim

Locks, bars on windows, and alarm systems are all useful devices to prevent unwanted intruders from making entrance into our homes and places of work. But what happens if an innocent victim is confronted with an invader who succeeds in entering his home, for example, and the safety of his family and possessions is now threatened? What if the invader confronts these innocent occupants and threatens some form of violence, including life-threatening force? What are the victims to do?

Critics of the Second Amendment and private gun ownership never seem to have any reasonable answer. Silent prayer might be suggested, but if this were to be a formal recommendation by the government it might run the risk of violating the separation of church and state.

Even in an era promoting equality among the sexes, it nonetheless remains a fact that on average an adult man tends to be physically stronger than an adult woman, and most especially if there is more than one man confronting a single woman.

Several years ago, economist Morgan Reynolds wrote a book on the economics of crime. The following is from one of the criminal cases he discussed. It seems that four men broke into a house in Washington, D.C., looking for a man named "Slim." When the occupant said that he didn't know where Slim was, they decided to kill him instead. One of the defendants later testified,

> "I got a butcher knife out of the kitchen. We tied him up and led him to the bathroom. And we all stabbed him good. Then, as we started to leave, I heard somebody at the door. Lois [the dead man's girlfriend] came in.... We took her back to the bathroom and showed her his body. She started to beg, 'don't kill me, I ain't gonna tell nobody. Just don't kill me.' She said we all could have sex with her if we wouldn't kill her. After we finished with her, Jack Bumps told her, 'I ain't takin' no chances. I'm gonna

kill you anyway.' He put a pillow over her head, and we stabbed her till she stopped wiggling. Then we set fire to the sheets in the bedroom and went out to buy us some liquor."

Would either of these two victims have been saved if the man had had a gun easily reachable by him in the house or if the woman had had a gun in her purse? There is no way of knowing. What is for certain is that neither was any match for the four men who attacked and killed them with a butcher knife. Even Lois's begging and submitting to sexual violation did not save her. How many people might be saved from physical harm, psychological trauma, or death if they had the means to protect themselves with a firearm?

Equally important, how many people might never have to be confronted with attack or murder if potential perpetrators were warded off from initiating violence because of the uncertainty that an intended victim might have the means to defend him- or herself from thieves, rapists, and murders? A gun can be a great equalizer for the weak and the defenseless, especially if an intended victim doesn't have to waste precious seconds fumbling with the key to a mandatory trigger lock.

But what is an ordinary man to do when he finds that it is the government that is the perpetrator of violence and aggression against him and his fellow citizens? How do you resist the power of the state? Tens of millions of people were murdered by governments in the twentieth century. They were killed because of the language they spoke or the religion they practiced. Or because those in political control classified them as belonging to an "inferior race" or to a "social class" that marked them as an "enemy of the people." Furthermore, the vast, vast majority of these tens of millions of victims were murdered while offering little or no resistance. Fear, terror, and a sense of complete powerlessness surely have been behind the ability of governments to treat their victims as unresisting lambs brought to the slaughter.

But part of the ability of government to commit these cruel and evil acts has been the inability of the victims to resist because they lacked arms for self-defense. However, when the intended victims have had even limited access to means of self-defense it has shocked governments and made them pay a price to continue with their brutal work.

The Power of Armed Resistance

Many have been surprised by the lack of resistance by the European Jews who were killed by the millions in the Nazi concentration and death camps during the Second World War. For the most part, with a seemingly peculiar fatalism, they calmly went to their deaths with bullets to the back of the head or in gas chambers. Yet when some of the people were able to gain access to weapons, they did resist, even when they knew the end was most likely be the same. The following is from historian John Toland's biography of "Adolf Hitler," in reference to the resistance of the Jews in the Warsaw Ghetto in 1943:

> "Of the 380,000 Jews crowded into the Warsaw ghetto, all but 70,000 had been deported to the killing centers in an operation devoid of resistance. By this time, however, those left behind had come to the realization that deportation meant death. With this in mind, Jewish political parties within the ghetto finally resolved their differences and banded together to resist further shipments with force . . .
>
> "At three in the morning of April 9, 1943, more than 2000 Waffen SS infantryman — accompanied by tanks, flame throwers and dynamite squads — invaded the ghetto, expecting an easy conquest, only to be met by determined fire from 1500 fighters armed with weapons smuggled into the ghetto over a long period: several light machine guns, hand grenades, a hundred or so rifles and carbines, several hundred pistols and revolvers, and Molotov cocktails. Himmler had expected the action to take three days but by nightfall his forces had to withdraw.
>
> "The one-sided battle continued day after day to the bewilderment of the SS commander, General Jürgen Stroop, who could not understand why 'this trash and subhumanity' refused to abandon a hopeless cause. He reported that, although

his men had initially captured 'considerable numbers of Jews, who are cowards by nature,' it was becoming more and more difficult. 'Over and over again new battle groups consisting of twenty or thirty Jewish men, accompanied by a corresponding number of women, kindled new resistance.' The women, he noted, had the disconcerting habit of suddenly hurling grenades they had hidden in their bloomers . . .

"The Jews, he reported, remained in the burning buildings until the last possible moment before jumping from the upper stories to the street. 'With their bones broken, they still tried to crawl across the street into buildings that had not yet been set on fire.... Despite the danger of being burned alive the Jews and bandits often preferred to return into the flames rather than risk being caught by us.' ... For exactly four weeks the little Jewish army had held off superior, well-armed forces until almost the last man was killed or wounded."

In the end the Germans had to commit thousands of military personnel and in fact destroy an entire part of Warsaw to bring the Jewish ghetto resistance to an end.

What if not only the Jewish population but the majority of all the "undesirable" individuals and groups in Germany and the occupied countries of Europe had been armed, with the Nazi government unable to know who had weapons, what types, and with what quantity of ammunition? It would be an interesting study in World War II history to compare private gun ownership in various parts of Europe and the degree and intensity of resistance by the local people to German occupation.

Revolts Against Tyranny

In the early years of the Bolshevik takeover in Russia there were numerous revolts by the peasantry against Communist policies to collectivize the land or seize their crops as in-kind taxes. What made this resistance possible for many years was the fact that in the countryside the vast majority of the rural population owned and knew how to use hunting rifles and other weapons of various kinds.

Acquisition of firearms during the Second World War as part of the partisan movement against the German invasion of the Soviet Union enabled active, armed resistance by Lithuanian and Ukrainian nationalist guerrillas against Soviet reoccupation of their countries to continue in the forests of Lithuania and western Ukraine well into the early 1950s.

It is hard to imagine how the people of the 13 colonies could have ever obtained their independence from Great Britain at the end of the eighteenth century if the local population had not been "armed and dangerous." It is worth recalling Patrick Henry's words in arguing for resistance against British control before the king's armed forces could disarm the colonists:

> "They tell us . . . that we are weak — unable to cope with so formidable an adversary. But when shall we be stronger? . . . Will it be when we are totally disarmed, and when a British guard shall be stationed in every house? . . . Three million people, armed in the holy cause of liberty . . . are invincible by any force which our enemy can send against us."

The taking up of arms is a last resort, not a first, against the intrusions and oppressions of government. Once started, revolutions and rebellions can have consequences no one can foretell, and final outcomes are sometimes worse than the grievance against which resistance was first offered. However, there are times, "in the course of human events," when men must risk the final measure to preserve or restore the liberty that government threatens or has taken away.

The likelihood that government will feel secure in undertaking infringements on the freedoms of Americans would be diminished if it knew that any systematic invasion of people's life, liberty, and property might meet armed resistance by both the victim and those in the surrounding areas who came to his aid because of the concern that their own liberty might be the next to be violated.

Though it may seem harsh and insensitive, when I read the advocates of gun control pointing to incidents of private acts of violence against children, I think to myself:

How many more tens of thousands of children were killed around the world in the last century by governments? And how many of those children, victims of government-armed violence, might have been saved if their families and neighbors had possessed the right to bear arms against political aggressors? How many children have been saved because their families have had weapons for self-defense against private violators of life and property? And how many could have been saved from private aggressors if more families had owned guns?

Guns and American Liberty

Nor should the argument that virtually all other "civilized" countries either prohibit or severely restrict the ownership and the use of firearms in general and handguns intimidate Americans. America has been a free and prosperous land precisely because of the fact that as a nation we have chosen to follow political and economic avenues different from those followed by other countries around the world.

As a people, we have swum against the tide of collectivism, socialism, and welfare statism to a greater degree, for the most part, than have our western European cousins. As a result, in many areas of life we have remained freer, especially in our market activities, than they. The fact that other peoples in other lands chose to follow foolish paths leading to disastrous outcomes does not mean that we should follow in their footsteps.

America was born in revolt against the ideas of the "old world": the politics of monarchy, the economics of mercantilism, and the culture of hereditary class and caste. America heralded the politics of representative, constitutional government, the economics of the free market, and the culture of individualism under equality before the law. It made America great.

If in more recent times there has been an "American disease," it has been our all-too-willing receptivity to the European virus of political paternalism, welfare redistribution, economic regulation and planning, and the passive acceptance of government control over social affairs.

We need not and indeed should not fall victim to one more of the European ailments: the disarming of the people under the dangerous notion that the private citizenry cannot be trusted and should not be allowed to have the means of self-defense against potential private and political aggressors in society. Let us stand apart once more and not fall prey to the false idea that somehow our European cousins are more enlightened or advanced than we on the matters of gun ownership and control. They are not.

Instead let us remember and stay loyal to the sentiment of James Madison, the father of the US Constitution, who praised his fellow countrymen when he said, "Americans [have] the right and advantage of being armed—unlike citizens of other countries whose governments are afraid to trust the people with arms."

Let us remain worthy of Madison's confidence in the American people and defend the Second Amendment of the Constitution upon which part of that confidence was based.

Periodical and Internet Sources Bibliography

The following articles have been selected to supplement the diverse views presented in this chapter.

Caroline Ballard, "Why Is It So Hard to Talk About the Second Amendment?" KUER, September 3, 2019. https://www.kuer.org/post/why-it-so-hard-talk-about-second-amendment#stream/0.

Russell Berman, "Where the Gun-Control Movement Goes Silent," *The Atlantic*, March 1, 2018. https://www.theatlantic.com/politics/archive/2018/03/guns-second-amendment-repeal/554540/.

Patrick Blanchfield, "The Brutal Origins of Gun Rights," The New Republic, December 11, 2017. https://newrepublic.com/article/146190/brutal-origins-gun-rights.

Alexia Fernandez Campbell, "I Went to a Huge Conference on School Safety. No One Wanted to Talk About Gun Control," Vox, July 30, 2018. https://www.vox.com/2018/7/30/17518970/school-shooting-solutions-safety.

CBS News, "Trump Vows to Protect Second Amendment as Gun Debate Continues," September 13, 2019. https://www.cbsnews.com/news/trump-vows-to-protect-second-amendment-as-gun-debate-continues/.

Steve Chapman, "Why the Second Amendment Is Irrelevant," *Chicago Tribune*, February 23, 2018. https://www.chicagotribune.com/columns/steve-chapman/ct-perspec-chapman-second-amendment-20180223-story.html.

Roland Hughes, "US Gun Debate: Four Dates that Explain How We Got Here," BBC News, August 5, 2019. https://www.bbc.com/news/world-us-canada-42055871.

Elie Mystal, "It's Time to Repeal—and Replace—the Second Amendment," The Nation, August 7, 2019. https://www.thenation.com/article/repeal-second-amendment-gun-control/.

Igor Volsky, "James Madison Played Politics and Gave Us the Second Amendment," Daily Beast, May 20, 2019. https://www.thedailybeast.com/james-madison-played-politics-and-gave-us-the-2nd-amendment.

OPPOSING
VIEWPOINTS®
SERIES

CHAPTER 4

How Should the Problem of Mass Shootings Be Addressed?

Chapter Preface

There is no "one size fits all" solution to eliminate mass shootings any time soon. But several solutions have been suggested in the hope that they would serve to lessen the number that have befallen American society since the 1999 Columbine massacre launched an era of horrifying tragedies.

Only one answer has been widely agreed upon by the American public. Surveys have shown that nearly all favor comprehensive background checks for all gun purchases. Yet Congress has not succeeded to even pass that legislation. That failure proves the power of the National Rifle Association (NRA), a tremendously influential lobbying group that has refused to back any measure that would limit access to guns.

Another popular tact would be an assault weapons ban, which had been in effect from 1994 to 2004 before expiring. Several mass shooters have since used assault weapons to gun down victims. The NRA continued to fight against restrictions on assault weapon access.

The NRA and millions of Americans who back gun rights have formed opposite opinions to those advocating gun control. They claim the spate of mass shootings can be slowed through a proliferation of guns. They embrace the theory that only well-meaning people with guns can stop those with bad intent.

Most Americans agree that mental health issues also must be addressed. But most mass shooters have not been diagnosed with mental imbalance, and some exhibited no threat to society before committing their heinous attacks.

One demand has been made by nearly all concerned citizens. That is, *something* must be done. Millions of people have grown angrier at the inaction of government officials. Americans are hoping for a safer future. They believe that doing nothing will ensure that mass shootings will continue unabated.

> *"Research has shown that gun-toting independence unleashes much more chaos and carnage than heroism. A 2017 National Bureau of Economic Research study revealed that right-to-carry laws increase, rather than decrease, violent crime."*

"Good Guys with Guns" Are Not the Solution

Susanna Lee

In the following viewpoint, Susanna Lee argues that the NRA has repopularized the theory of the "good guy with a gun." This character was popularized in cheap literature dating back nearly a century but resurfaced during a 2012 speech made by NRA chief executive Wayne LaPierre. The author believes the view that only a good guy with a gun can stop a bad guy with a gun is a fantasy peddled by the NRA and other gun rights advocates, and many Americans have bought it hook, line, and sinker. Lee cites studies and statistics to further her view that the theory has no basis in reality. Susanna Lee is a professor of French and comparative literature at Georgetown University.

As you read, consider the following questions:

1. Which pieces of fiction from the first half of the twentieth century does the author use to prove the origins of the "good guy with a gun" theory?

2. Does the author make a strong argument that the theory is a weak one?

3. What evidence does the author use to argue that the theory can be considered racist?

At the end of May, it happened again. A mass shooter killed 12 people, this time at a municipal center in Virginia Beach. Employees had been forbidden to carry guns at work, and some lamented that this policy had prevented "good guys" from taking out the shooter.

This trope—"the good guy with a gun"—has become commonplace among gun rights activists.

Where did it come from?

On Dec. 21, 2012—one week after Adam Lanza shot and killed 26 people at Sandy Hook Elementary School in Newtown, Connecticut—National Rifle Association Executive Vice President Wayne LaPierre announced during a press conference that "the only way to stop a bad guy with a gun is a good guy with a gun."

Ever since then, in response to each mass shooting, pro-gun pundits, politicians, and social media users parrot some version of the slogan, followed by calls to arm the teachers, arm the churchgoers, or arm the office workers. And whenever an armed citizen takes out a criminal, conservative media outlets pounce on the story.

But "the good guy with the gun" archetype dates to long before LaPierre's 2012 press conference.

There's a reason his words resonated so deeply. He had tapped into a uniquely American archetype, one whose origins I trace back to American pulp crime fiction in my book "Hard-Boiled Crime Fiction and the Decline of Moral Authority."

Other cultures have their detective fiction. But it was specifically in America that the "good guy with a gun" became a heroic figure and a cultural fantasy.

"When I Fire, There Ain't No Guessing"

Beginning in the 1920s, a certain type of protagonist started appearing in American crime fiction. He often wore a trench coat and smoked cigarettes. He didn't talk much. He was honorable, individualistic—and armed. These characters were dubbed "hard-boiled," a term that originated in the late 19th century to describe "hard, shrewd, keen men who neither asked nor expected sympathy nor gave any, who could not be imposed upon." The word didn't describe someone who was simply tough; it communicated a persona, an attitude, an entire way of being.

Most scholars credit Carroll John Daly with writing the first hard-boiled detective story. Titled "Three Gun Terry," it was published in *Black Mask* magazine in May 1923.

"Show me the man," the protagonist, Terry Mack, announces, "and if he's drawing on me and is a man what really needs a good killing, why, I'm the boy to do it."

Terry also lets the reader know that he's a sure shot: "When I fire, there ain't no guessing contest as to where the bullet is going."

From the start, the gun was a crucial accessory. Since the detective only shot at bad guys and because he never missed, there was nothing to fear.

Part of the popularity of this character type had to do with the times. In an era of Prohibition, organized crime, government corruption, and rising populism, the public was drawn to the idea of a well-armed, well-meaning maverick—someone who could heroically come to the defense of regular people. Throughout the 1920s and 1930s, stories that featured these characters became wildly popular.

Taking the baton from Daly, authors like Dashiell Hammett and Raymond Chandler became titans of the genre.

Their stories' plots differed, but their protagonists were mostly the same: tough-talking, straight-shooting private detectives.

In an early Hammett story, the detective shoots a gun out of a man's hand and then quips he's a "fair shot—no more, no less."

In a 1945 article, Raymond Chandler attempted to define this type of protagonist:

> Down these mean streets a man must go who is not himself mean, who is neither tarnished nor afraid. … He must be, to use a rather weathered phrase, a man of honor, by instinct, by inevitability, without thought of it, and certainly without saying it.

As movies became more popular, the archetype bled into the silver screen. Humphrey Bogart played Dashiell Hammett's Sam Spade and Raymond Chandler's Philip Marlowe to great acclaim.

By the end of the 20th century, the fearless, gun-toting good guy had become a cultural hero. He had appeared on magazine covers, movie posters, in television credits and in video games.

Selling a Fantasy

Gun rights enthusiasts have embraced the idea of the "good guy" as a model to emulate—a character role that just needed real people to step in and play it. The NRA store even sells T-shirts with LaPierre's slogan, and encourages buyers to "show everyone that you're the 'good guy'" by buying the T-shirt.

The problem with this archetype is that it's just that: an archetype. A fictional fantasy.

In pulp fiction, the detectives never miss. Their timing is precise and their motives are irreproachable. They never accidentally shoot themselves or an innocent bystander. Rarely are they mentally unstable or blinded by rage. When they clash with the police, it's often because they're doing the police's job better than the police can.

Another aspect of the fantasy involves looking the part. The "good guy with a gun" isn't just any guy—it's a white one.

In "Three Gun Terry," the detective apprehends the villain, Manual Sparo, with some tough words: "'Speak English,' I says. I'm none too gentle because it won't do him any good now."

In Daly's "Snarl of the Beast," the protagonist, Race Williams, takes on a grunting, monstrous immigrant villain.

Could this explain why, in 2018, when a black man with a gun tried to stop a shooting in a mall in Alabama—and the police shot and killed him—the NRA, usually eager to champion good guys with guns, didn't comment?

A Reality Check

Most gun enthusiasts don't measure up to the fictional ideal of the steady, righteous and sure shot.

In fact, research has shown that gun-toting independence unleashes much more chaos and carnage than heroism. A 2017 National Bureau of Economic Research study revealed that right-to-carry laws increase, rather than decrease, violent crime. Higher rates of gun ownership is correlated with higher homicide rates. Gun possession is correlated with increased road rage.

There have been times when a civilian with a gun successfully intervened in a shooting, but these instances are rare. Those who carry guns often have their own guns used against them. And a civilian with a gun is more likely to be killed than to kill an attacker.

Even in instances where a person is paid to stand guard with a gun, there's no guarantee that he'll fulfill this duty.

Hard-boiled novels have sold in the hundreds of millions. The movies and television shows they inspired have reached millions more.

What started as entertainment has turned into a durable American fantasy.

Maintaining it has become a deadly American obsession.

> *"Citizens stop active shooters less often than the police do, but it's crystal clear that armed citizens have saved lives. They've stopped massacres that would have further plunged American families and American communities into deep grief."*

You Too Can Be a Good Guy with a Gun

David French

In the following viewpoint, David French uses several recent examples of mass shooting tragedies to argue in favor of the "good guy with a gun" theory. The author believes that citizens who carry a gun can prevent tragedies. He also contends that many proposed anti-gun legislation measures have been deemed ineffective. In addition, he encourages readers to take up arms and think of themselves as potential do-gooders in similar dangerous situations. David French is an author and former senior writer for the National Review.

"In Missouri, a Good Guy with a Gun Stepped Up—So Can You," by David French, *National Review*, August 9, 2019. Reprinted by permission.

As you read, consider the following questions:

1. How realistic is the "good guy with a gun" solution in stopping mass shootings before they start?
2. How does the author address the notion of preventing bad guys from getting guns?
3. How does the author encourage readers to eliminate their fears in a potentially dangerous situation?

Yesterday, a terrifying scene played out in a Walmart in Springfield, Mo. A man pulled up to the store, donned body armor, and armed himself with a "tactical rifle," a handgun, and more than 100 rounds of ammunition. He walked into the store and began recording himself on his phone as he pushed a shopping cart. The moment, complete with the video, had echoes of mass shootings from Christchurch to El Paso to Dayton.

Panicked customers fled, and the police sped toward the store, but by the time they arrived, the crisis had passed. A private citizen described as a "former firefighter" had pulled his firearm and was holding the man at gunpoint. That thing that supposedly never happens just happened again. A good guy with a gun averted a potential crisis.

We don't yet know the intentions of that heavily armed young man, but there are other recent incidents where we do know the criminal intent—where the shooting had already started—and men with guns intervened to save lives. But we tend to forget the attacks that are frustrated or foiled, and we always seem to forget the heroes who saved lives.

For example, you may be able to instantly recall the names of at least four or five mass shooters, in spite of your best efforts to forget them. But here are two men we should remember—Bryan Whittle and Juan Carlos Nazario. They heard the "popping of gun shots" at a popular Oklahoma City restaurant, they grabbed their weapons, moved toward the danger, engaged the shooter, and killed him.

Have we already forgotten the name of Jonathan Morales, the armed citizen who (along with an unarmed man named Oscar Stewart) engaged the synagogue shooter in Poway, Calif.? I'd imagine that not even the most dedicated gun-rights supporter can remember the non-massacre at Schlenker Automotive in Rockledge, Fla. There, the shooter killed one man and wounded another before two employees of the store—Don Smith and Nathan Taylor—returned fire, wounded the shooter, and held him at gunpoint until the police arrived.

I could go on. The FBI has recorded no fewer than 19 times in a five-year span (and that estimate may be low)—from 2014 to 2018—when active shooters were stopped or repelled by citizens. Seven times armed citizens stopped the shooting entirely. Twice an armed citizen engaged the shooter and caused him to flee the scene. Citizens stop active shooters less often than the police do, but it's crystal clear that armed citizens have saved lives. They've stopped massacres that would have further plunged American families and American communities into deep grief. They've stopped massacres that would have further polarized American politics.

It's easy to feel helpless in the face of the mass-shooting contagion, especially when the disease is spreading and legislative solutions appear so elusive. For example, the RAND Corporation examined studies of the effects of 13 popular gun-control proposals—including "bans on the sale of assault weapons and high-capacity magazines"—and "found no qualifying studies showing that any of the 13 policies we investigated decreased mass shootings."

But feeling helpless is different from being helpless. When you purchase a weapon, train yourself to use it effectively, and obtain a carry permit, you are making an important declaration—the place where you are is instantly less vulnerable. An active shooter in your presence will face resistance.

Carrying a weapon is not a casual decision. Responsible gun owners don't just do the minimum the law requires—buy the weapon, take the concealed-carry class, and then slide the gun into their holster and forget about it. Responsible gun owners train. They go to the range. They learn how to handle their weapon with a kind of prudent confidence, recognizing both the power of the gun and their mastery of a potent tool.

No person knows—until the fateful moment comes—if you'll respond with the bravery of Don Smith, Nathan Taylor, Jonathan Morales, Bryan Whittle, or Juan Carlos Nazario. We find (or lose) our courage at times of ultimate testing. But one thing you can do—you can prepare to be brave.

Here's the bottom line. Regardless of your frustration at national politics and regardless of your sense of frustration at social forces that feel are out of your control, you can do something about mass shootings. You can defend yourself. You can defend the people you love. And that's exactly what you should train yourself to do.

> "There is no gun registration, gun ban, or gun confiscation that a US Congress can pass and a US president can sign that will be even close to fully complied with or enforced."

Gun Buybacks Are Futile

Jon Stokes

In the following viewpoint, Jon Stokes argues that the notion of a massive gun buyback to eliminate such weapons from the American streets is unrealistic. Gun buyback programs allow gun owners to trade their firearms to law enforcment or another government entity in exchange for cash or other items of value. The author feels that those who own guns are generally passionate about defending themselves and would push back hard against any laws that mandated confiscation. He cites the AR-15 as a weapon that owners would be hard-pressed to give up. The author also cites previous attempts at buybacks to prove what he perceives as a failure to achieve their purpose. Jon Stokes is a gun rights advocate and contributing editor at TheFirearmBlog.com.

"The Futility of a Gun Buyback," by Jon Stokes, Reason Foundation. Reprinted by permission.

As you read, consider the following questions:

1. Does the author offer any better solutions to gun violence than buybacks?
2. How does the author chastise the media for its reaction to buyback proposals?
3. Why does the author bring marijuana and immigration laws into his argument?

Gun bans are back in the news again, with the 2020 Democratic field lining up behind the (old, already-tried-and-failed) idea of a ban on the AR-15, the AK-47, and any other gun that looks remotely "military."

The most aggressive recent version of this proposal was floated by a certain Texan who's currently sinking in the polls, and it includes a mandatory buyback. When asked if he plans to actually take away people's guns, Beto O'Rourke replied: "I want to be really clear that that's exactly what we are going to do. Americans who own AR-15s, AK-47s, will have to sell them to the government."

Meghan McCain's response to O'Rourke on *The View*—"if you're talking about taking people's guns from them, there's going to be a lot of violence"—and Tucker Carlson's subsequent pile-on (that it'll spark a "new Civil War") sent the usual suspects straight to the fainting couch, pearls in hand.

Media Matters has already put out two pieces on the remarks, one focused on Carlson and a breathless followup focused more generally on "right-wing media" reactions to the proposed gun ban. *HuffPost* reporter Zach Carter accused McCain of "mainstreaming apocalyptic thinking." (One wonders what he thinks of HuffPost headlines like "Are We Heading Toward Extinction?") *Crooks & Liars* amped everything up another notch by claiming Carlson's rhetoric about the danger of gun confiscation is itself dangerous.

Before we go any further with the back-and-forth about armed resistance, let's think about the reaction we can realistically expect to a watered-down AR-15 ban, with no mandatory buyback. How many gun owners would either hand over or destroy their assault weapons? And how many of the authorities whose job it would be to put refusers in jail would even try to enforce a ban?

We don't have to look to New Zealand's recent flop of a mandatory buyback, where less than 10 percent of the country's estimated number of newly banned weapons have been handed over so far, to answer those questions. There's a great case study right here in the bluest of blue states: New York.

Gov. Andrew Cuomo hailed the 2013 New York SAFE Act as the toughest gun control law in the nation, and one of its most important provisions was the mandatory registration of all "assault weapons" in the state. This isn't a confiscation or even a ban, so it's nowhere near as severe as what O'Rourke and others are pushing— it's just a teeny weeny little registration requirement.

So how has that worked out? Well, according to the National Shooting Sports Foundation's conservative estimate, New Yorkers owned about 1 million "assault weapons" at the time the ban was passed. So the 44,000 that were actually registered are about 4 percent of the total. This noncompliance with the law is widespread and mostly open, but the police aren't doing much about it. For instance, *Hudson Valley One* reported in 2016:

> Upstate police agencies have also demonstrated a marked lack of enthusiasm for enforcing the ban on assault weapons and large-capacity magazines. According to statistics compiled by the state Department of Criminal Justice Services, there have been just 11 arrests for failure to register an otherwise-legal assault weapon since the SAFE Act took effect in March 2013 and 62 for possession of a large capacity magazine. In Ulster County, where 463 assault weapons have been registered, there have been just three arrests for possession of large-capacity magazines and none for failure to register an assault weapon. Ulster County Sheriff Paul VanBlarcum has been a vocal critic of the law; he said he believed large numbers of Ulster County gun owners had chosen to ignore the registration requirement.

I could give several more examples of such reporting. But the upshot is that gun owners are overwhelmingly ignoring the law—and the police are overwhelmingly looking the other way.

A 2017 article from NYU law professor James Jacobs sums up the state of play. After detailing the electoral damage the backlash against the act did to New York Dems—"In 2014, Governor Andrew Cuomo was reelected by a much diminished majority and Republicans regained control of the State Senate"—Jacobs concludes that the "SAFE Act's impact on gun crime, suicides and accidents has never been seriously assessed, although both gun control proponents and gun rights advocates make extravagant claims. **In truth, there seems little likelihood that the SAFE Act has had much, if any, effect since it has been only partially implemented, almost completely unenforced, and widely ignored. Its various provisions are easily circumvented"** (emphasis mine).

New Yorkers are famous for their attitude, but this local police pushback on state and federal gun laws is not at all limited to New York. Nor is it a recent development. In 2013, for example, NBC reported on local sheriffs from Maryland to Colorado who publicly touted their refusal to enforce any gun laws they feel infringe on the Constitution. The growing Second Amendment Sanctuary movement, active in California, New Mexico, Oregon, and a handful of other states, is being led by local law enforcement.

If you're one of my many pro–gun control friends, you're no doubt offended at the spectacle of local police officials and city governments flat-out refusing to enforce democratically legislated marijuana laws…sorry, I mean immigration laws…oops, I mean gun laws.

I totally get that. When I read a quote like the following, there is indeed a part of me that thinks that if this radical insurrectionist loves cops and hates democracy this much, then maybe he should move to Hong Kong: "When [a prominent politician] kind of goes after these phantom sanctuary cities and talks about how bad they are, basically what he's going after is police chiefs. And I trust police chiefs, in terms of knowing what should be done to keep their communities safer, and police departments and mayors, a lot more than I trust [that Washington politician]."

Oh, no—I got mixed up again. That was former Democratic vice presidential nominee Tim Kaine, in a 2016 CNN interview on the topic of immigration sanctuary cities, and the politician he was criticizing is Donald Trump.

My point, other than the fact that hypocrisy around federalism is depressingly bipartisan, is not that it's either good or bad for local cops to veto laws. My point is that regardless of what you think of the gun owners who won't comply or the cops who'll inevitably let them off without even a verbal warning, there is no gun registration, gun ban, or gun confiscation that a US Congress can pass and a US president can sign that will be even close to fully complied with or enforced. Not one.

That isn't a boast or a threat. It's just a prediction, and a fairly safe one.

So the question I have for everyone who still wants to go down this road is this: What will you do in the face of the inevitable mass noncompliance? What is your Plan B?

Is the next step increased penalties for lawbreakers? If so, then how will you catch these lawbreakers in order to penalize them if the cops aren't interested in going after them?

Is your plan to go after the police, then? Would you declare war on any local sheriffs and even state police who ignore the law? If this stood a realistic chance of happening, you'd think they'd do it in New York, of all places. But a lot of that state's cops have been openly ignoring the country's "toughest" gun law, and we've heard crickets.

Or maybe you plan to escalate to door-to-door confiscation as a last resort.

In that case, I think Meghan McCain's prediction of violence is about as safe as my prediction of mass noncompliance and law enforcement nullification. There would probably be a lot of ugliness and not a few dead bodies, not to mention a massive waste of the political capital of any party pushing the police into a shooting war with even a relatively small number of AR-15-owning bitter enders.

Even if you think gun owners are bluffing and will hand 'em over peacefully when the time comes, you'd risk a violent escalation of America's worsening culture war solely for the sake of outlawing a category of weapons that are involved in the low triple-digits of US deaths in any given year? Really?

This doesn't seem rational to me. It seems more like the kind of culture-war red meat you throw out there when you're trying to revive a flagging presidential campaign.

> *"Right-to-carry laws, whether open or concealed, tend to increase violent crime. A 2019 study found that right-to-carry laws 'are associated with 13–15 percent higher aggregate violent crime rates 10 years after adoption.'"*

Open Carry Is Wrong Law for Curbing Gun Violence

Paul Ausick

In the following viewpoint, Paul Ausick rails against those that believe in universal open carry laws. Ausick cites a 2016 mass shooting in Dallas in which the sheer number of people in the area openly carrying guns made it difficult for police to identify the shooter. The author also notes a study conducted a year later that found that the presence of gun-toting people in the streets can cause others to behave more aggressively. Ausick supports this theory with statistics. Paul Ausick is a senior editor at 24/7 Wall Street.

"Do Open Carry Laws Increase or Decrease Gun Violence?" by Paul Ausick, 24/7 Wall St., August 12, 2019. Reprinted by permission.

As you read, consider the following questions:

1. What evidence does the author provide that open carry laws do not limit mass shootings?
2. Why have some retail stores banned guns in open-carry states?
3. How does the author use statistics to make his case?

Sometime in the past 10 years or so, all of us have heard or read the remark, "The only thing that stops a bad guy with a gun is a good guy with a gun." National Rifle Association (NRA) Executive Vice President Wayne LaPierre uttered the phrase barely a week after the school shooting at Sandy Hook Elementary School in Newton, Connecticut, that killed 27 children and educators. LaPierre was arguing that to protect the nation's children, the country needed to station an armed police officer in every US school.

Law enforcement officers are, almost by definition, the good guys, but a fair inference from LaPierre's statement is that any good citizen with a gun can stop an armed bad one. There is anecdotal evidence of that.

Another possible inference to be drawn from LaPierre's statement is that carrying a gun is (or should be) legal. Of the 50 states and the District of Columbia, only six ban open carrying of a handgun (California, the District of Columbia, Florida, New York and South Carolina), and only seven ban open carrying of long guns (rifles and shotguns), according to data from the Giffords Law Center. They are California, the District of Columbia, Florida, Illinois, Massachusetts, Minnesota and New Jersey.

Another 20 either require a permit to openly carry a handgun or place some other restriction on open carrying in public places. Only five states (Iowa, Pennsylvania, Tennessee, Utah and Virginia) restrict, but do not prohibit, open carrying of long guns.

In states with open carry laws, law enforcement agencies may not be able quickly to distinguish a real threat from a legal open carry. At a 2016 mass shooting in Dallas in which five police officers were shot and killed, the presence of some 30 people legally carrying long guns made it difficult for police to sort the good guys from the bad.

Unlike laxer open carry rules, carrying a concealed weapon generally requires a state-issued permit in 35 states, while 15 states have no restrictions on concealed carry. Only eight of the 35 states that require permits have enacted what are called "may issue" laws, which grant state authorities wide discretion to deny a concealed carry permit to an applicant. In the other 27 states, authorities "shall issue" a concealed carry permit, and 14 of those the states allow no discretion to the permit-issuing authority.

Note that a 2017 study found that merely seeing a gun can increase aggression. The researchers noted, "[O]ur naïve meta-analytic results indicate that the mere presence of weapons increased aggressive thoughts, hostile appraisals, and aggression, suggesting a cognitive route from weapons to aggression."

Right-to-carry laws, whether open or concealed, tend to increase violent crime. A 2019 study found that right-to-carry laws "are associated with 13–15 percent higher aggregate violent crime rates 10 years after adoption." Another study reported in 2017 found that "shall-issue" laws were "significantly associated with 6.5% higher total homicide rates, 8.6% higher firearm homicide rates, and 10.6% higher handgun homicide rates, but were not significantly associated with long-gun or nonfirearm homicide."

While state laws vary widely, there is one nationwide law that limits open or concealed carrying of firearms. In a federal circuit ruling known as GeorgiaCarry.Org Inc. v. Georgia, the court ruled the right to bear arms granted by the Second Amendment to the US Constitution does not supersede a "fundamental" right to exclude arms from private property. That means that businesses may legally ban firearms and other weapons from their premises. Full stop.

Stores like Target, which in 2014 "respectfully request[ed]" its shoppers to leave their guns at home received heated blowback from some gun owners, have persevered. Others, like Walmart, which itself sells guns in its US stores, have allowed customers to carry guns openly in states where open carry is legal. But Walmart is somewhat of an exception. Gun sales policies have been changing in the country—these are the big American retailers that don't sell guns.

CNBC has posted a list of unusual places where people can bring a gun. These include most churches (except in some states where concealed carry in churches is banned), casinos in most states, bars and restaurants, most airports (but not airplanes), voter registration and polling places, hospitals, national parks, libraries and several others.

In addition to Target, guns have been banned at cinema chains like AMC, Carmike and Cinemark; eateries like Buffalo Wild Wings, Hooters and Starbucks; and at dozens, if not hundreds, of shopping malls across the country. Simon Property Group, which owns or holds an interest in more than 200 US shopping malls, does not allow firearms at its malls.

Of the 100 largest US retailers last year, just seven sold firearms of any kind. A new study out earlier this year from researchers at Boston University found that the kind of gun control that is most likely to work is one specific type, and it has nothing to do with banning weapons.

> *"You go into the community with preventive resources. You do your best to lower the background levels of bullying and discrimination. You track the data and perform what is called 'threat assessments' on potential risks."*

Focus on Prevention Instead of Reacting

Anya Kamenetz

In the following viewpoint, Anya Kamenetz argues that having guns in schools, particularly in the hands of teachers, will not prevent mass shootings. The author contends that vigilance and monitoring of mental health and acting on possible threats against students and faculty is the most effective way to stop tragedies from occurring. Kamenetz takes a step-by-step approach in giving school officials a method to identify and stop potential shooters. Anya Kamenetz is National Public Radio's education correspondent.

"Here's How to Prevent the Next School Shooting, Experts Say," by Anya Kamenetz, National Public Radio Inc. (NPR), March 7, 2018. Reprinted by permission.

As you read, consider the following questions:

1. Do most or all potential school shooters give clues as to their plans, according to the viewpoint?
2. Did the author effectively frame the steps required to identify and stop possible perpetrators?
3. Does the author explain why she is against arming teachers?

After Parkland, there have been many calls to make schools a "harder target"—for example, by arming teachers. But there's a decent amount of research out there on what actually makes schools safer, and most of it doesn't point to more guns.

On the Friday after the deadly shootings at Marjory Stoneman Douglas High School in Florida, Matthew Mayer, a professor at the Rutgers Graduate School of Education, got an email during a faculty meeting.

The email was from Shane Jimerson, a professor at the University of California, Santa Barbara. Both specialize in the study of school violence.

That email led to nearly two weeks of long days, Mayer says, for some of the leading experts in the field. On conference calls and in Google docs they shaped a concise, eight-point "Call for Action To Prevent Gun Violence In The United States of America."

About 200 universities, national education and mental health groups, school districts, and more than 2,300 individual experts have signed on to support this document in the weeks since.

Their topline message: Don't harden schools. Make them softer, by improving social and emotional health.

"If we're really talking about prevention, my perspective is that we should go for the public health approach," says Ron Avi Astor at the University of Southern California, who also helped draft the plan.

A public health approach to disease means, instead of waiting for people to be rushed to emergency rooms with heart attacks or the flu, you go into the community: with vaccinations, screenings, fruits and vegetables, walking trails and exercise coaches. You screen and regulate environmental hazards, like a nearby polluting factory. You keep watch on reported cases of illness, to stop a new outbreak in its tracks.

A public health approach to school shootings, Astor explains, would be much along the same lines.

Instead of waiting for people to, again, be rushed into emergency rooms, you go into the community with preventive resources. You do your best to lower the background levels of bullying and discrimination. You track the data and perform what is called "threat assessments" on potential risks.

And, these experts say, you remove the major "environmental hazard" that contributes to gun violence: the guns. The eight-point plan calls for universal background checks, a ban on assault-style weapons, and something called Gun Violence Protection Orders: a type of emergency order that would allow police to seize a gun when there is an imminent threat.

What sets this call to action apart from other policy proposals is not gun control, however, but the research-based approach to violence prevention and response. This is a long haul, say the experts, not a quick fix.

"No matter what you try to do by just hardening the target, we've learned that having the armed officers isn't necessarily going to stop it," says Matthew Mayer at Rutgers. "Having the metal detector or the locked doors isn't going to stop it. The hard work is a lot more effort. You'd better start thinking in a more comprehensive manner about prevention instead of reacting."

Prevention: The First Step

School climate may sound fuzzy or abstract. It means the quality of relationships among the students and the adults in a school. It's affected by the school's approach to discipline and behavior, the availability of professionals like counselors and social workers, as well as any social-emotional curriculum taught in the classroom.

STOP SCAPEGOATING THE MENTALLY ILL

After the horrific event of a mass shooting in the US, it takes time for details of the perpetrator to emerge. But without fail, their violent criminal record, any ties to radical extremism, the legality of weapons they used, and their mental health history are the first things scrutinized by the media, policy makers, and the general public.

However, one of these details is not like the others—mental health histories should not be linked to a propensity to commit a mass shooting. There is no evidence that indicates a person with a mental health condition is any more likely to participate in senseless violence than anyone else. In fact, people with mental health conditions are more than 10 times more likely to be victims of violent crime than the general population.

It is not yet clear whether the perpetrators of the massacres in Las Vegas last month and in Sutherland Springs this week had mental health conditions, and while the Texas shooter spent time in a behavioral facility following assault charges, to blame his long history of violence on a mental health condition would be reductive. And yet President Donald Trump described the cause of Sunday's tragedy as a "mental health problem," ignoring the myriad issues that have stronger correlations to gun violence. For example, more than 50 percent of people who commit mass shootings have a history of domestic violence. Yet mental health history is cited much more often.

Instead of thoughtlessly blaming mental health conditions for every act of mass violence, we should look at the facts: the use of a gun by someone with mental health condition is more likely to result in suicide than assault.

Scapegoating people who are already stigmatized based on their mental health won't end gun violence. While solutions to stopping mass shootings are long overdue, real progress won't come at the cost of perpetuating false stigma, fear, and unfounded discrimination against people with disabilities.

"Mental Health Scapegoated in US Gun Control Debates," Human Rights Watch.

School climate, in turn, affects students' mental and emotional health and academic success. And research by Astor and others has consistently found key factors that can make schools safer: cultivate social and emotional health, connect to community resources and respond, particularly, to troubled students.

Why does this matter? Well, for one thing, the very kids who bring weapons to school are more likely to report being bullied or threatened themselves. They may be fearful of gang violence and feel a need to protect themselves on the way back and forth to school.

Or, they may be individually ostracized and aggrieved. This is true not just in the United States, says Astor, but in "Kosovo, Canada, Chile, Israel, the kids who bring weapons to school are reporting tons of victimization."

So, if you devote resources to shutting down bullying, discrimination and harassment, there is a chance to de-escalate conflict before it starts.

And research shows that school climate measures really work. In fact, there has been a steady downward trend in bullying and harassment over the past decade, which Catherine Bradshaw at the University of Virginia attributes in part to evidence-based social and emotional measures.

The Witnesses

There is a second reason a better school climate can cut down on violence. It's what Astor refers to as the role of the witness.

He again cites the example of California, which does a comprehensive annual survey. There, 20 to 30 percent of students above the elementary level consistently report seeing a weapon of some kind at school at least once during the year. That's conservatively more than half a million students, just in that one state.

Moreover, based on the survey, at least 125,000 of these students in California were actually threatened or injured by a weapon on school grounds. This includes things like knives and nunchuks as well as guns.

But what happens next?

If that witness, or that victim, has a strong relationship with an adult, they are more likely to report being menaced by a weapon. Whereas, if there is what Astor calls a "no snitching culture" in the school, or the witness fears for their safety, nothing will be done.

He says he's not urging schools to punish or expel the kid who brought the weapon, but, instead, to use "education as an intervention."

This approach is applicable not only for mass shootings, he says, but for violence that arises from disputes between students or when gang violence in the community spills onto school grounds.

And, he says preventing gun violence also means looking at suicide. Suicide is just behind homicide as a leading cause of death for teenagers. When a weapon comes to school, self-harm may be the plan, and a school-climate approach addresses that threat as well.

The researchers' policy plan calls for assessing school climate nationwide; reducing "exclusionary practices" like suspension and expulsion; maintaining physically and emotionally safe schools; and staffing up with specialists like counselors, psychiatrists, psychologists and social workers, both in the school and in the community.

Emergency Mode

While school climate is an ongoing background effort, the public health approach has an emergency mode when it comes to violence. It kicks in when someone does report a person bringing a weapon to school or talking about violence. It's called a "threat assessment."

After the Columbine shooting in 1999, the FBI and the Secret Service each conducted studies of school shootings and shared their knowledge with the nation's educators. They found that there was no one "profile" of a school shooter. But, almost all students who committed homicide had told someone of their intentions.

So, the two law enforcement agencies recommended that schools copy what the Secret Service does when someone makes a threat on a government official. Threat assessment has been required by law in Virginia's schools since 2013, and adopted in many other places.

A threat assessment team consists of the principal, school counselor, school psychologist and a school-based police officer. They talk to the people involved and any witnesses. They try to figure out if the threat is serious: Is it specific? Is there a detailed plan? Is there a weapon?

In a school, the next steps include notifying parents, taking steps to protect victims, and referrals to mental health and law enforcement if appropriate.

Threat assessments are not a fail-safe. A local ABC affiliate in Florida did report, based on school records, that a threat assessment was ordered for Parkland shooting suspect Nikolas Cruz, based on an incident that happened in January 2017, a year before the shooting.

But Dewey Cornell at the University of Virginia, another author of the Call to Action, says researchers have gathered good evidence to support the technique, when implemented fully as in Virginia. Among the positive impacts, he says, are "reduced suspensions and reduced bullying, students and teachers reporting that they feel safer, and students reporting a greater willingness to report threats of violence."

His research also shows that less than 1 percent of threats are ever carried out.

The researchers are hopeful that their Call to Action will break through the noise. But they've been here before, Mayer says. A group of his colleagues wrote something similar in 2012 after the shootings at Sandy Hook Elementary School, and after a group of school shootings in 2006. Mayer hopes, this time, people will be paying attention.

Periodical and Internet Sources Bibliography

The following articles have been selected to supplement the diverse views presented in this chapter.

Bruce Bower, "Are Researchers Asking the Right Questions to Prevent Mass Shootings?" Science News, August 9, 2019. https://www.sciencenews.org/article/are-researchers-asking-right-questions-prevent-mass-shootings.

Melissa Chan, "Three Businesses Say They've Got What You Need to Survive a Mass Shooting," *Time*, October 18, 2019. https://time.com/5698423/bulletproof-backpacks-school-shootings/.

Ellen Cranley, "How to Stop Shootings in America; 10 Strategies Proposed to Stop Gun Violence, and How Likely They Are to Work," *Business Insider,* August 5, 2019. https://www.businessinsider.com/how-to-stop-gun-school-shooting-america-2018-11.

Everytown, "Keeping Our Schools Safe: A Plan to Stop Mass Shootings and End Gun Violence in American Schools," February 11, 2019. https://everytownresearch.org/reports/keeping-schools-safe-plan-stop-mass-shootings-end-gun-violence-american-schools/.

Sean Gregory and Chris Wilson, "6 Real Ways We Can Reduce Gun Violence in America," *Time*, March 22, 2018. https://time.com/5209901/gun-violence-america-reduction/.

Tara Haelle, "Want to Stop Mass Shootings: Do These Two Things, Physician Says," Forbes, September 27, 2018. https://www.forbes.com/sites/tarahaelle/2018/09/27/want-to-stop-mass-shootings-do-these-two-things-physician-says/#2786e5cb5501.

Alex Hannoford, "We Asked 12 Mass Killers: 'What Would Have Stopped You?'" GQ, September 12, 2018. https://www.gq-magazine.co.uk/article/mass-shootings-in-america-interviews.

Nicole Hockley, "Four Out of Five Mass Shooters Give You the Power to Stop Them," Quartz, August 9, 2019. https://qz.com/1684180/how-to-stop-mass-shootings-before-they-happen/.

Megan Kamerick, "Preventing Mass Shootings," The Whole Story, November 1, 2018. https://thewholestory.solutionsjournalism.org/preventing-mass-shootings-d9ab6c3c3177.

For Further Discussion

Chapter 1

1. Why has there been such a huge increase in mass shootings since 1999?
2. What has been the biggest failure of the United States in combating gun violence since the turn of the century?
3. How do the views of Donald Trump differ from those of other recent US presidents regarding school shootings?

Chapter 2

1. Why do some people feel an assault weapons ban would prove ineffective? Use examples from the viewpoints in this resource to support your case.
2. Should the United States work toward a gun-free society? Why or why not?
3. Given that strong gun control laws work in other countries, why do many people argue that they would not have the desired effect in America?

Chapter 3

1. Should the Second Amendment be still considered viable today? Why or why not?
2. What changes, if any, should be made to the Second Amendment to better deal with changes in society and upgrades in the danger level of weapons?
3. How should the "well-regulated militia" part of the Second Amendment be interpreted?

Chapter 4

1. How effective can Americans be in preventing mass shootings through understanding mental health warnings signaled by potentially dangerous people?
2. What is the one most effective change in US policy that can have the most significant impact on gun violence?
3. Are open carry laws a viable deterrent to mass shootings?

Organizations to Contact

The editors have compiled the following list of organizations concerned with the issues debated in this book. The descriptions are derived from materials provided by the organizations. All have publications or information available for interested readers. The list was compiled on the date of publication of the present volume; the information provided here may change. Be aware that many organizations take several weeks or longer to respond to inquiries, so allow as much time as possible.

American Civil Liberties Union (ACLU)

125 Broad Street, 18th floor
New York, NY 10004
(212) 549-2500
email: aclupreferences@aclu.org
website: www.aclu.org

The American Civil Liberties Union uses its resources to fight for and preserve individual rights and freedoms in the United States. The ACLU believes in gun rights but has worked to impose reasonable limits on firearms sales and ownership.

Americans for Responsible Solutions

PO Box 15642
Washington, DC 20003-0642
email: info@americansforresponsiblesolutions.org
website: giffords.org

This nonprofit and political action committee was founded by shooting victim and former US congresswoman Gabby Giffords and husband Mark Kelly after the Sandy Hook massacre in 2012. It raises money to help elect politicians that favor and work toward sensible gun control measures.

Brady Campaign

840 1ˢᵗ Street NE, Suite 400
Washington, DC 20002
(202) 370-8100
email: bradyunited.org/contact
website: www.bradyunited.org

The Brady Campaign works for comprehensive gun reform. Included among its targets are stronger background checks, limiting gun purchases, taking weapons of war off the streets, restricting bump stocks, and funding urban programs that fight gang violence.

Center for American Progress

133 H Street NW
Washington, DC 20005
(304) 285-5704
email: www.americanprogress.org/about/contact-us
website: www.americanprogress.org

A focus on solving the mass shooting crisis and gun violence in America in general is one of many missions of this organization. The Center for American Progress works to push the United States forward in a progressive direction.

Centers for Disease Control and Prevention (CDC)

1600 Clifton Road
Atlanta, GA 30329-4027
(800) 232-4636
email: https://wwwn.cdc.gov/dcs/contactus/form
website: https://www.cdc.gov/violenceprevention/
youthviolence/schoolviolence

The CDC has worked in more recent years to prevent school violence, which includes bullying, fighting, cyberbullying, weapons use and gang violence.

Coalition to Stop Gun Violence

805 15th Street NW
Washington, DC 20005
(202) 408-0061
email: csgv@csgv.org
website: www.csgv.org

The mission of the nation's oldest gun violence prevention organization is developing policies, as well as community engagement and training that will help end mass shootings and other gun-related deaths. The CSGV seeks to draft, pass, and implement gun legislation based on research and evidence.

Everytown for Gun Safety

(646) 324-8250
email: everytown.org/contact-us
website: www.everytown.org

Along with subsidiary Moms Demand Action for Gun Sense in America, this group serves as a counter to the National Rifle Association by advocating for a legislative agenda. This includes stronger background checks and keeping guns away from domestic abusers. It also backs more stringent anti-trafficking laws for dangerous weapons.

National Association for Gun Rights

PO Box 1776,
Loveland, CO 80539
(877) 405-4570
email: https://nationalgunrights.org/contact-us/
website: www.nationalgunrights.org

This conservative organization take a no compromise approach to gun rights and against gun control advocates. It seeks to hold anti-gun politicians accountable for their views while preserving the Second Amendment.

National School Safety Center

30200 Agoura Road, Suite 260
Agoura Hills, CA 91301
(805) 373-9977
email: info@schoolsafety.us
website: www.schoolsafety.us

Established in 1984, the National School Safety Center serves as an advocate for safe, secure, and peaceful school settings. Among the missions of the organization is to prevent crime and violence in schools. It helps provide training at schools intended to prevent tragedies.

Project Mobilize

7674 W. 63rd Street
Summit, IL 60501
email: www.mobilize.org/join-the-movement
website: www.mobilize.org

Project Mobilize features a group of leaders that seek millennials to foster positive change within the system and through existing organizations. It also works to invest in new ideas that would help unify Americans in a progressive manner on a variety of issues such as gun control.

Protect Our Schools

7674 W. 63rd Street
Summit, IL 60501
email: http://protectourschools.com/#take-action
website: www.protectourschools.com

This organization combines the concern and work of students, teachers, parents, and community activists to take action against gun violence in schools. The website provides many ways that people can help, including through the ballot box.

Sandy Hook Promise

(203) 304-9780
email: https://www.sandyhookpromise.org/contact-us
website: www.sandyhookpromise.org

Dedicated to the victims of the Sandy Hook school massacre, this organization works to create a culture that prevents shootings, violence, and other harmful acts in schools.

Second Amendment Foundation

12500 Northeast 10th Place
Bellevue, WA, 98005
(425) 454-7012
email: info@saf.org
website: www.saf.org

The goal of SAF is to inform the public about their rights and educate people about its views of the gun control debate.

Students Against Violence Everywhere (SAVE)

(866) 343-SAVE
email: nationalsave.org/contact
website: https://nationalsave.org

SAVE Promise clubs seek young advocates to create safer schools and communities across the country to prevent potentially tragic outcomes.

Youth Over Guns

PO Box 3354
New York, NY 10163
(212) 679-2345
email: info@youthoverguns.org
website: www.youthoverguns.org

Youth Over Guns provides members an opportunity to become politically and socially active with a platform to become agents of change.

Bibliography of Books

Amye Archer and Lauren Kleinman, eds. *If I Don't Make It, I Love You: Survivors in the Aftermath of School Shootings.* New York, NY: Skyhorse Publishing, 2019.

Ken Baumgarten. *Arguing About Guns: The All-American Debate.* Independently published, 2019.

Jennifer Carlson. *Citizen-Protectors: The Everyday Politics of Guns in an Age of Decline.* New York, NY: Oxford University Press, 2015.

Philip J. Cook and Kristin A. Goss. *The Gun Debate: What Everyone Needs to Know.* New York, NY: Oxford University Press, 2014.

Firmin DeBrabender. *Do Guns Make Us Free? Democracy and the Armed Society.* New Haven, CT: Yale University Press, 2015.

Matt Doeden. *Gun Violence: Fighting for Our Lives and Our Rights.* Minneapolis, MN: Twenty-First Century Books, 2019.

Thomas Gabor. *Confronting Gun Violence in America.* New York, NY: Palgrave Macmillan, 2016.

David Hemenway. *Private Guns, Public Health.* Ann Arbor, MI: University of Michigan Press, 2017.

Albert Jack. *Gun Control USA: The NRA: Why Mass Shootings in America Won't Stop.* Albert Jack Publishing, 2015.

Peter Langman, *School Shooters: Understanding High School, College, and Adult Perpetrators.* New York, NY: Rowman & Littlefield, 2017.

Michelle Roehm McCann. *Enough Is Enough: How Students Can Join the Fight for Gun Safety.* New York, NY: Simon Pulse/Beyond Words, 2019.

Andrew Pollock and Max Eden. *Why Meadow Died: The People and Policies That Created the Parkland Shooter and Endanger America's Students*. Brentwood, TN: Post Hill Press, 2019.

Mario Robertson. *Second Amendment: The Risk of Repeal*. North Conway, NH: Waterhouse Publishing, 2018.

Jaclyn Schildkraut. *Mass Shootings in America: Understanding the Debates, Causes, and Responses*. Santa Barbara, CA: ABC-CLIO, 2018.

Ranjit Singh and Greg Camp. *Each One, Teach One: Preserving and Protecting the Second Amendment in the 21st Century and Beyond*. CreateSpace Independent Publishing Platform, 2016.

Bradley Steffens. *Gun Violence and Mass Shootings*. San Diego, CA: ReferencePoint Press, 2018.

Christopher Street. *Gun Control: Guns in America, the Full Debate, More Guns Less Problems? No Guns No Problems?* CreateSpace Independent Publishing Platform, 2016.

Michael Waldman. *The Second Amendment: A Biography*. New York, NY: Simon & Schuster, 2015.

Whitman Publishing. *Legally Armed: Carry Gun Law Guide*. Florence, AL: Whitman Publishing, 2017.

Index